Most Likely To Summon

Nyhiloteph

Most Likely To Summon Nyhiloteph

Madison McSweeney

This is a work of fiction. **Any similarity to actual persons, living, dead, undead, or actual events is purely coincidental.**

@littleghostsboo 

@littleghostsbooks 

Published by Little Ghosts Books.

Visit us at littleghostsbooks.com

Little Ghosts Books is committed to protecting the environment. The entirety of this book, the cover as well as the interior, is printed on acid-free 100% recycled fibers within Canada.

Cover Designed and illustrated by Chris Krawczyk.

Edited by Chris Krawczyk

ISBN: 978-1-7389097-4-2

Also by Madison McSweeney:

The Forest Dreams With Teeth

(Demain Publishing, 2021)

The Doom That Came to Mellonville

(Filthy Loot, 2021)

Fringewood

(Alien Buddha Press, 2022)

Beach Vibes

(Anuci Press, 2024)

Most Likely To Summon Nyhiloteph

Part I:

I'll Kill You If You Don't Come Back

Chapter 1

Attending your own funeral isn't as fun as you might assume. Living people have this obsession with hearing what people really think of them, or at least all the nice things that they hope their friends are too embarrassed to say to their faces. But once you die, people start lying about you.

Here were my parents, grasping at straws, talking about dreams I'd never realize. My father telling everyone how excited I'd been to study journalism, a program I'd only applied to because an English degree seemed impractical. My mother describing a generosity of spirit I hadn't displayed since I was a young child. They might as well have been making up stories about shadows.

At least their grief was honest. Not like some of my snot-faced classmates, sobbing not because they missed me but because my death forced them to contemplate their own mortality. Or my least favourite teachers, talking about me in fortune cookie platitudes; how thoughtful I was, how spirited.

All the performative mourning couldn't steal the show from my real friends, fresh from the fatal collision. Abdul, who never played a sport more physical than the Math Olympics, looked like he'd survived a boxing match. Brady, perpetually blissfully stoned, now stoned but far from blissful. And Jackson, our unofficial leader, the man with the plan and the driver's license – the man who got us t-boned by a BMW running a red – looked deader than me. I'd never seen him in a suit and tie. I'd also never seen a human being look so grey.

I was shocked when they took my parents' place at the podium. Leaning on each other (except for Abdul, who shrugged off physical contact) they looked like a scrappy friend gang from a coming-of-age movie, minus the obligatory girl for the female demographic. I guess that used to be me.

Jackson was opening his mouth to speak when something pinched me. I slapped my arm, where the sting was strongest, but the sensation merely shifted. Left arm, shoulder, cheek, stomach. Not pain, per se; it was more like someone pulling at folds of my skin. My head felt hollow, like a beach ball was expanding inside my skull, crowding out my brain and threatening to burst.

Can dead people be sick, in danger? Shit, can we die again?

More likely: I'd exhausted my time on earth was finally being called into the afterlife. And right before the main event. That's it, Lucy. You'll never graduate high school, shop for dorm room furniture, make out with a hot girl at a keg party. Anything else you've neglected to do?

Little black dots gathered in front of my eyes. When I tried to lift my arm to rub them out, I could barely move; it was like being buried in quicksand. I used the last of my free will to fling myself at the podium, for one last goodbye that no one would be able to hear.

That's when I unravelled.

Chapter 2

You know that scene in *Hellraiser* in which the villain gets pierced with dozens of hooks, before the unseen Cenobites yank their chains and rip him apart? This was like that. Or like when you fill a balloon too full and it pops as you're trying to tie it. No longer able to withstand the force, my spirit flew though the cosmos like shrapnel.

When I re-materialized, the first thing I saw was a horned owl surrounded by a halo of fire, orange eyes piercing mine. I reeled backward, bumping my head against the ceiling. The owl didn't stir.

Taxidermy. The luminescence was from lit candles, arranged haphazardly alongside religious figurines and an array of sparkling, monolithic crystals. We were in the top corner of a dingy room, the owl and the icons on a mounted shelf, me dangling like a spider. All but one wall were velvet curtains. Old lightbulbs under red lampshades gave the place a fiery glow, dancing shadows masking layers of dust.

Voices drew my gaze downward, to the man and woman hunched over a circular table. She was in her late sixties at least, grey hair dyed purplish and gaudy costume jewellery on her skeletal wrists and fingers. The man was younger; one of those guys who could be twenty-five or forty-five and you wouldn't be surprised either way. He wore grey chinos, sneakers that had seen better days, and one of those black t-shirts with twin wolves on them. On the table between them was a crystal ball.

The man's chin flicked up, his grey-green eyes boring into mine. "I sense a presence here."

The lady's head flitted to every nook and shadow of the room, as if scanning for signs of infestation. At last, she followed his eyes to my corner, landing on me without seeing me. She was trembling with grief, or terror, or anticipation- I couldn't tell.

"Is that you, Warren?"

I'd heard the woman fine, but the man repeated the question. "Is the spirit of Warren Schenedsky in this room with us?"

"No," I said, and heard my voice for the first time since my death.

The words weren't audible, but they felt like sound, producing the same vibrations in my throat and in the room that my voice would have made. Up until this point, my words had been empty air, like trying to speak with laryngitis.

The medium's back stiffened. He'd heard me, too, and he didn't like the answer. Eyebrow arching, he glanced edgily at his client. "What is your name, spirit?"

I couldn't take my eyes off the woman, eyes damp with restrained tears, hope and anguish ready to overflow.

"What's your name?" I stalled. "And where are we?"

"My name is Artemis," the medium replied. "And this is Helen Schenedsky. We're in my store, The Grimoire, in Ottawa. Canada."

Ottawa, Canada? I thought. Wasn't that obvious? Where was this Warren guy from? That explained it - the ghost they were looking for wasn't from here. He was too far away, and Artemis's seance had just snatched up the nearest spirit. Me.

"I could be Warren," I relented, pitying Helen.

Artemis grinned and stifled it. "The spirit is a bit confused. But I think it's him."

Helen was beaming. Whoever Warren had been, he'd meant everything to her.

"Tell her I love her," I wracked my brain for something personal but generic, feeling like a fortune cookie writer. "And that our wedding day was the happiest of my life."

When Artemis relayed the message, Helen's smile twisted into a scowl. "Warren was my grandson."

Artemis's jaw dropped.

"This is just terrible, taking advantage of a grieving grandmother. Do you have a grandmother, young man?"

"Uhhh..."

"I bet you do. Would you want someone to do this to her, if you were dead? Which would be well-deserved, to be frank."

Helen nearly ripped the curtain down as she stormed from the séance room and into the lobby of a small bookstore. The floorboards squeaked and sagged, squealing even more loudly when Artemis ran after her.

"And don't think I'm paying for this!" she exclaimed before stomping down the stairs, her oversized purse knocking over the sandwich board on the stoop.

Artemis waited until she was down the street before venturing out to fix the sign. I immediately recognized the storefront. It was a place I'd known as "the old abandoned house" as a child, a greying wooden building that must have been a nice home in its day, situated on a street that my mother used to call, "the lane of lost dreams." This was the last edge of developable land before the neighbourhood was lost to woods. The street had been designed for residential use, but the lots were too close to wildlife to be desirable to young families. This house had become The Grimoire, the yellow bungalow next to it became a chiropractor's office, and so on.

Artemis grimaced as he bent over the downed sign; I felt the flare of pain in his knees and concluded that I didn't envy the way he moved through the world. The hinges pinched his fingers as he righted the board, which read: "Yes, I can help you speak to the dead! Enquire inside."

Always money to be made conning grieving widows, I thought. But at least Artemis's powers were real, if too unfocused to be useful. Yes, I can help you speak to the dead- but it's just Lucy.

Unfortunately, I knew someone in the market for exactly that type of conference.

Chapter 3

Outbound ghostly communication is extremely hit or miss, which makes it maddening that I can perceive almost everything. Sometimes that takes the form of involuntary mind reading – if someone's thinking loudly enough, I can hear it, though rarely with the full context. But mostly, it's picking up vibes. Fear, anxiety, anger. I can almost smell them. That's why I could tell that Jackson was not doing well in the aftermath of the crash. Depression stinks like rotting fruit.

Having nothing better to do, I would go to his house and find him in bed at noon, not even sleeping, just staring at the popcorn ceiling. I'd overhear his parents arguing about whether they should give him space or push him to return to the world: final exams were coming up, his university acceptance was contingent on those grades, Lucy wouldn't have wanted him to throw his future away, etc.

I wanted nothing more than to talk to Jackson and tell him the same thing. But that seemed to be against the rules.

I've always been protective, admittedly to a fault, sometimes bordering on jealousy. Most of my life I'd gone through friends like socks, the people I hung out with fluctuating based on who I had classes or clubs with, shyness preventing me from deepening the connection. That all changed in senior year. When I started hanging out with Jackson and Brady and Abdul, I felt like I'd finally found my people, and I didn't want that to change.

All this is to say, I did what I did with the best of intentions.

I left breadcrumbs leading to the Grimoire, but Jackson was slow to follow them. It took me knocking a business card from Artemis's desk and brandishing it across town via gusts of wind before Jackson realized he was receiving a sign. And then he spent three days ruminating on it, twirling the card between his fingers and running his fingertips across the text, before he actually went to Artemis's. I followed him there from his house, nudging him when he made a wrong turn until he couldn't miss the place.

Classic Jackson, he picked the absolute worst afternoon for an outing. It was one of those days that just screamed rain from daybreak. Hot clouds churned high overhead, grey and ominous, the air stinking with humidity. The storm held off until he was halfway to the store, then drenched the world in an instant. Luckily Jackson didn't turn back.

He looked confused as he stepped inside. Optimistically, I'd figured he would see the sign advertising Artemis' medium services and connect the dots. Instead, he aimlessly circled the displays, wondering why he was even there. Artemis's skulls and masks posed the same question, sizing him up with hollow eyes.

"Can I help you?" Artemis asked, tone so rude I wondered how he stayed in business.

"Just looking around," Jackson said, spinning again, his dripping clothes making puddles on the floorboards.

"Ask him about speaking to the dead!" I cried. Not even the medium heard me this time.

That's when I noticed the sandwich board leaning against one of the walls, tucked out of sight next to the door. Artemis must have brought it in from the storm. Fuck.

Jackson flipped through a magazine at random, realized it was all about embalming techniques, and returned it to the shelf. I panicked as he eyed the door. If he left now, I was all out of options. Using all the spectral strength I had, I plucked a book from a display table and chucked it across the room. It hit the sign with a thud and a clatter, flipping the board around so the text faced out. *Yes, I can help you speak to the dead!* Ever-helpful, Jackson rushed to the site of the disturbance. But his eyes skipped right over the ad as he picked up the book.

It was only then that I saw its title: *Communing with Spirits: A Layman's Guide to Summoning from the Beyond.*

My bloodless heart sank. "Don't overcomplicate things," I warned.

He approached the cash. "Pardon me - how much is this going for?"

Artemis narrowed his eyes, taking the book from him as if to look for a price tag he knew wasn't there. It was incredibly old, pages onion-skin thin, oxblood leather cover close to falling apart. "What do you want it for?"

Jackson hesitated before settling on the truth. "I lost a friend recently. It was a car accident and I was driving. I just want to talk to her one more time."

"You can do that here!" I screamed, wanting to shake Artemis. Surely, he would take the opportunity to promote his own services.

A fourth presence entered the store. I felt it in the sudden chill, like someone had walked in from a blizzard and brought the cold in with them. But no one had come through the door.

It was a male presence, and big, though I saw nothing with my eyes. Artemis seemed to feel it, too, because his back stiffened. A deep, hollow voice boomed through the room: For you, it's free.

Jackson, the only one of us who hadn't heard, watched expectantly. "*For you, it's free,*" Artemis said, and handed the book back to him. "You should leave now, I'm closing up."

I saw Jackson check his watch and wonder what kind of store closes at 3:22 PM. But he did what he was told.

"And don't come back," the medium muttered, once the door between them shut.

The walls and floors shook violently as the spectre laughed.

Chapter 4

Jackson gathered the friend group under the pretence of food court Chinese food. The competing noises of a hundred shopping-bag-rustling, wrapping-paper-tearing, loud-chewing patrons allowed them to speak without being overheard. Jackson waited until the grease-stained box of chicken balls was half-empty and everyone had eaten a spring roll before he pushed the dishes aside and laid the book in the centre of the table.

"Is this Latin?" Abdul asked, wiping sweet and sour sauce off his fingers with a napkin. "How are we supposed to read this?"

"I Google translated the instructions," Jackson said, pulling a sheaf of printouts from his backpack. "I think you have to recite the spell in Latin, but it's phonetic, right?"

Abdul nudged the book away from his plate, as if its leather binding might still carry some contagious disease of the flesh. "Where did you even find this?"

"Yeah, man." Brady's fingers twitched, like they wished they were rolling a joint. "How do you know it's legit?"

"That's the thing," Jackson said. "I got it in this weird bookstore near the woods. You know that house with the skeleton on the roof?"

"I think that's a chiropractor's office," Abdul said.

"Next door to that," Jackson corrected. "You have to see the place, it's spooky as hell. I don't even know how I found it, it was like someone was leading me there, you know? And when I was looking around, this book just flew off the shelf. Like I was supposed to find it. It was like – like Lucy wanted me to find it."

The invocation of their dead friend cast a shadow over the table.

Abdul blinked. "Dude, you sound like you've lost your mind."

"I know," Jackson admitted. "But you weren't there."

"You seriously think this could bring Lucy back?" Brady asked, prodding the spongy binding with his finger. "How? Like, is she gonna dig herself out of her grave, all rotted and–"

"Stop." Red-faced, Jackson shoved the pages back into his bag. A toddler at the next table looked over in concern. "This is stupid, I shouldn't have suggested it."

Brady placed a hand on his shoulder. "Sorry. I didn't mean it like that."

"No, you're both right. I'm being crazy. I just..."

Brady squeezed tighter, not letting him go. "You're not being crazy. And if you really wanna do this, of course we'll help."

"I didn't agree to that!" Abdul interrupted. "I don't think this is a good idea at all!"

Brady took Abdul aside, colliding with a flock of KFC-bound teens as they made their way to a pillar near the entrance. The crowd was sparser here, and they were out of Jackson's earshot. "Come on, you know this isn't actually gonna work. Why not humour him?"

"Yeah, and then what?" Abdul asked. "Nothing will happen, and he'll be more depressed than he is already."

Brady whipped off his tuque, scratched his scalp, and re-hatted. "Something might. Maybe he'll feel a warm gust of wind that reminds him of her, or a butterfly'll land on him and he'll see it as a message from beyond. I don't know. But what we've been doing so far hasn't been working for him. Maybe this will."

"A creepy evil ritual from a leatherbound book?"

"What, you a vegan now? Come on, you know he'd do something like this for you if you asked."

"That's the thing," Abdul said. "I wouldn't ask."

You didn't have to be an undead mind-reader to see the fight had left him. Brady wrapped Abdul in a headlock, knuckling his hair as he squirmed out. "It'll be fine. We'll do a little witchy shit, cheer Jackson up. It'll fail miserably. One day it'll be nothing but a funny story. Good?"

"Fine."

"Rad. Let's go tell Jackson we're in."

The boys overstayed the food court's sixty-minute limit, whispering around the table even as the mall emptied and employees shuttered their shops. They were supposed to be discussing the ritual, but Brady got distracted and talked circles around it.. Abdul was quiet, examining the translated printouts.

"You know, my cousin was into Wicca," Brady announced, shovelling cold forkfuls of ginger beef into his mouth. "Or whatever it's called. She learned about it from a Scooby Doo movie, at least that's what she told her parents because they were threatening to throw out her Evanescence CDs. I don't know if they were actually scared of it, I think her dad was just annoyed by all the scented candles..."

The book lay untouched, eavesdropping. Though I was glad no one was stroking it reverently, I wished one of them would at least pay some attention to it, because then they would see that it was breathing, the leather expanding and contracting ever so slightly.

"Jack," Abdul interrupted, holding the sheets close to his face because he'd neglected to wear his glasses. "This recipe calls for a fetus."

Operation Fetus was too easy.

It was grade eleven dissection day, and several dozen fetal pigs were on the chopping block. I'd always hated that biology unit. Frog dissection was fine, but those half-formed pigs, tied down by their ankles with their bellies exposed looked almost like human babies.

At lunchtime, the science teacher left for the lounge, and the formaldehyde drenched specimens were unsecured. It was a quick in-out procedure, Jackson armed with half-assed excuse he didn't end up needing. Within minutes he was skulking down the hall with an insulated lunch bag full of unborn hog.

The bag looked unremarkable but reeked of pre-emptive death and unnatural preservation. The hallway branched off toward a set of double doors, from where he could beat a hasty retreat behind the portables and through the school's rear gate. Brady lived nearby, and once Jackson made it to his shed, he'd be safe. He made the ninety-degree turn without paying attention and smacked right into my killer.

The girl driving the Beamer that night was Adrienne de Keyser, daughter of real estate magnate Mark de Keyser and paediatric surgeon Dr. Eleanor de Keyser, hostess of opulent-for-our-age pool parties I was never invited to.

Classic, right? Rich, popular kid driving recklessly, kills the nobody nerd and gets away with it. Except Adrienne hadn't been drunk or texting or anything like that; she suffered a sudden onset seizure behind the wheel, some condition she didn't even know she had, and was now dealing with crushing guilt as well as some scary health stuff. I didn't even get the satisfaction of hating her.

She looked like she hadn't slept since the accident, thick mascara enhancing, not masking, the bags under her eyes. She flinched when she recognized Jackson, as if she was about to get hit, and Jackson, in that disarming way he had, said, "Hi."

"Hi," Adrienne replied, weighing every word she could possibly say. Finally, she decided on, "Are you going to Grad Oscars?"

Grad Oscars? The senior class's popularity contest awards assembly?

"I wasn't going to," Jackson said, thinking the same thing I was.

"I think they're giving Lucy an award," she said hurriedly. "Like, as a tribute? It's not official yet, I just…I was on the organizing committee, and…"

Jackson's mind was racing, trying to think of some way to extract himself from this; worrying that Adrienne could smell the pig; that even if she couldn't smell the pig, someone would notice it was missing and chase him down; not paying attention to anything Adrienne was saying; wishing she would wrap it up, then worrying that maybe he should be paying attention because it would look suspicious if she asked him a question and he didn't know what she'd been talking about. "What award are they going to give her?" he asked. "Most likely to what, exactly?"

Adrienne blushed. "I kind of recused myself from those conversations. I think it's something like 'Best Friend' or 'Most Missed.' It's kind of trivial, I guess."

"I think she'd like that," Jackson interrupted, going through the motions as he edged toward the double doors.

"I'd rather be recognized for something other than being crushed by a BMW," I said.

Adrienne sighed. "I'm glad."

"Good." Jackson took the beginning of a step.

"Hey," she exclaimed. "Now that we're talking…"

Jackson was taking deep nose-breaths, trying to assure himself that no smells had escaped the bag. "Yeah?"

"Do you want to be…involved? In the tribute? The Committee was actually looking to talk to some of Lucy's friends for ideas, but we didn't want to bug anyone after the…"

"You didn't want to bother the car accident people?"

"We just didn't want to put you guys through more…"

Pain. She couldn't even say it.

Jackson, as he always did, rushed to smooth over the discomfort. "I mean, if you want photos or stories about Lucy or something, I have…"

"You'd do that?" Adrienne asked. "I mean, it wouldn't be…?"

"She was my best friend," he insisted, just as the bag started to leak. He shoved his cell phone into her hand; Adrienne took forever to type her email into the address book while drops of chemical-scented water pooled at his feet.

Her nose crinkled as she handed back the phone. "Hey, what's in that bag?"

Dorky as fuck, Jackson blurted out, "That's on a need-to-know basis," and beelined for the doors.

Was that the hint of a smile forming on Adrienne's lips?

Chapter 5

And that's how the next few weeks went. I watched impotently as my friends gathered baby teeth and virgins' hair, shopped for cheap cauldrons on Amazon, counted down the days until the last waning moon on a calendar showing images from the Hubble Space Telescope. Jackson and Adrienne grew closer as they planned my tribute, which felt pleasingly like the plot of a rom-com. Maybe, I hoped, they'd heal each other and he'd forget about this dangerous remorse-driven scheme.

No luck. He drew a new X on that calendar every day.

And each day I tried to get through to him. But every time I got into the same room as Jackson or Brady or Abdul, a pair of huge hands wrapped around my throat.

One night after dark, Adrienne called Jackson and asked if she could come over. I joined, of course. I'd long disregarded the stigma against voyeurism; it was more important I keep an eye on the boys to keep them out of further trouble.

Adrienne didn't notice anything out-of-the ordinary as she peeled off her top, revealing a yellow lacey bra with underwire. As her jeans came off, I averted my eyes. That was when I got my first glimpse of the demon.

He never revealed himself to me directly, but the room stank of his arousal and I could see his reflection in the mirror. He was massive, forced to slouch even to fit into Jackson's high-ceilinged bedroom. His fur was black and bristly, shoulders wide and rounded, no neck; I thought he looked slightly like a porcupine. Between his legs, his dick was unbelievably huge, spiny like the rest of him and about as wide as a boa constrictor after a feeding.

As Adrienne fingered the band of her underwear, the penis lifted up. Without thinking I whisked a frame off Jackson's dresser and sent it careening towards the mirror. The glass smashed and the shards fell to the floor, taking the indecent image with them.

"What was that?"

Apologizing, Adrienne picked up the frame and turned it over to see how bad the crack was. Her face crumpled. Fuck me, it was a group photo of me and the guys. Smiling next to Daleks at Ottawa ComicCon.

"Are you okay?" Jackson asked.

"This isn't right," she stammered, gathering her clothes. I've never seen someone get dressed so fast, holding in tears all the while. She whipped the door open and wrestled her purse off the knob, trying to do every leaving-thing at once and slowing herself down in the process.

"Adrienne, what's wrong?"

She whirled around, her anguish becoming a scowl. "Are you really that clueless?" And then she was slamming the door and running down the stairs. Jackson stared at the blank wood, indeed clueless, no idea he'd been cockblocked by his dead best friend.

That night, I came to Artemis in a dream. I'd tried this trick on a zillion people, but he was the only one it worked on. I guess medium powers never sleep.

The dream took us to the woods, but not really. I could feel cold air on my arms but not the pine needles under my feet, and there was no smell to anything. It was like standing in front of a green screen. Artemis faced me, a blank expression on his face. I got the feeling he would tell me whatever I wanted to know. And I wanted to know what the deal was with that demon.

"Who was the spirit that appeared in the store?" I demanded. "Who told you to sell Jackson- er, that teenager- The Grimoire?"

"Nyhiloteph," Artemis replied, his eyes dreamy.

"Who is Nyhiloteph?"

"He's a magpie."

That didn't make sense to me, but I continued. "Why did he want Jackson to have the book?"

"Because he has dominion over it."

"How so?"

"The book has the power to summon the dead. If the ritual is done correctly, the subject of the spell will appear as they were in life. If the ritual is done incorrectly, it will summon Nyhiloteph."

"And what will he do then?"

The hypnotized Artemis shrugged. "Whatever he wants."

I remembered the huge, barbed hands around my throat and thought that Nyhiloteph seemed pretty powerful already. But maybe he could only touch me and other ghosts in his current state. Maybe he needed to be summoned if he wanted to mess around with the physical world.

"I have to warn Jackson," I said to myself. Ever notice in dreams, you have to say things out loud, instead of just thinking them?

I'd assumed from Artemis's detached tone that he was in some sort of trance, but it turned out he was just being condescending. He surprised me by replying, "Fat chance."

Chapter 6

The next day, when Adrienne returned to an empty math classroom to retrieve a forgotten textbook from her desk, I grabbed a piece of chalk and wrote on the blackboard: THIS IS LUCY.

It looked awful. My handwriting was even more jagged and terrible than it had been in life. I never understood how anyone could write nicely on a vertical surface.

Adrienne screamed and ran out of the room.

Now, this pissed me off. I realize she was truly not culpable for the accident – really, she was a victim herself - but I was the one who was dead, and if I wanted to talk to her, I darn well had the right to. So, after picking up the textbook and closing it neatly, I followed her down the hall.

I knew on instinct that she was about to duck into the girls' washroom, so I beat her to it. When she turned the corner, she was greeted by a message on the mirror, scrawled with a piece of red lipstick someone had left behind: DON'T TRY TO RUN FROM ME, BITCH.

Perhaps that was over the top.

Adrienne started to twitch and spasm. Holy shit, another seizure. She grabbed the edge of the counter to hold herself up, but her eyes rolled into the back of her head and she rolled with them, collapsing on the bathroom floor.

The moon waned tonight. We were doomed.

I spent the evening sulking in Artemis's shop, stroking the partridge mounted atop a corner bookshelf. Artemis noticed its feathers rippling and addressed me from behind the desk: "I sense you, presence. Reveal yourself." I flung a book at his head instead. He was bending to pick it up when the front door chimed.

Adrienne.

She looked totally out of place here. I think she would have turned around and walked back out had Artemis not greeted her, the sight of someone so young and female in the store startling him into politeness.

She walked to the desk, hands fidgeting with the strap of her purse, zebra print Kate Spade with a leather fringe tail. Like everything she wore, it was cute but classy. I'd died in an oversized RUSH t-shirt and was doomed to wear it for eternity.

"I…was hoping you could help me," she stammered, her eyes flicking around the store, trying to reassure herself that this was a legitimate place.

"With?"

Adrienne looked at the ground. The voice that came out of her mouth was small and choked: "I think I'm being haunted."

The bare bulb cast daunting shadows across the séance room, giving every lamp and table bending, elongated legs. The red tablecloth preventing the crystal ball's base from scratching the wood was askew; Adrienne stepped on it as she sat down, sending cloth and ball flying. Artemis barely caught it.

"Sorry," Adrienne said, lowering her eyes. "I've never done this before."

"I'm sure you've sat at a table," he retorted.

I studied Artemis as he went through the motions, somehow thinking I could gauge his trustworthiness just by watching. Ha. The only insights I gleaned were aesthetic: a certain pride of appearance, hindered by a lack of style or resources or both. His clothes were faded, t-shirt fraying at the seams, pants baggy around the knees. His brownish hair was cut in a lopsided imitation of a David Bowie shag, a self-haircut if I'd ever seen one. His teeth were clean and white but bent at odd angles, like he'd taken care of himself as best he could but someone at some critical period hadn't thought to get him braces. Or hadn't had the money. I wondered how he'd come to own a store.

His voice brought me back: "I sense a presence here." Adrienne's fists clenched for a fraction of a second.

Now that he'd phrased it that way, I did feel more present. I'd always been in the room with them, but now it was like I was back on their plane. Just like the first time I'd been summoned. Was this the sensation Nyhiloteph was chasing?

"I like your purse," I said to Adrienne, feeling like I could just make conversation again.

Artemis squinted. "It's a woman," he said skeptically. "She likes your purse."

Adrienne gasped. "Is it Lucy?"

"Spirit! Is your name–"

"Lucy, yes," I snapped. "And tell her I know she was having a seizure when she was driving and I'm not mad about that. But I have something important to tell her and she has to pay attention."

"It's Lucy," Artemis said. "She said she knows the accident wasn't your fault and she forgives you."

The look of relief on her face disgusted me, despite my best efforts to be charitable. Now was not the time for catharsis. "That's not the point!" I snapped, and the lightbulb flickered. Artemis winced like I'd slapped him.

Adrienne's teary eyes went wide. "What happened?"

"She has a message for you," Artemis said, rubbing his cheek.

"Thank you." I was about to give her the whole story – the book, the resurrection spell, Nyhiloteph – but stopped myself. Whatever Nyhiloteph was, Artemis knew and was afraid. "Jackson is about to do something he'll really regret, and you have to stop him," I explained, hoping that was vague enough. "I can't tell you what it is, but I can tell you where he'll be."

"When and where?" she asked, after Artemis had translated.

"The third clearing in the Old Quarry Trail. Where the burnouts always drink." I waited for Artemis to give her the location, but something made him hesitate. Fuck - did he suspect? Did Jackson's name tip him off? Or was he just waiting for me to finish?

Nothing else to do, I concluded: "At one past midnight under the waning moon. Tonight."

Artemis stood up, arms flailing, knocking over his own stool. "This session is over. Out, unclean spirit!" The exclamation flung me backward. I felt the connection to his mind sever as I hit the wall.

"What's going on?" Adrienne cried. "What did she say?"

"That wasn't your friend," Artemis lied. "That was a malign spirit trying to lead you to a very dangerous place."

"But what about Jackson? Is he okay?"

"None of that was true. This spirit is trying to fool you. You can't listen to anything she – it – says."

Adrienne continued to protest as he shooed her out of the séance room and closed the curtain. "But what do I do? Will the spirit come back?"

"I can't help you with this. Consult an exorcist."

I was roaring at this point, kicking up breezes and rattling shelves. Leather bound books tumbled to the ground and fell open to images of demonic orgies. All it did was spike Artemis's panic, and he hastened Adrienne toward the exit.

"But -"

"You have to leave. You've put me in enough danger already."

"You put yourself in danger, you snake oil selling fraud!" I spat.

Adrienne was halfway out the door, trying to push past Artemis to get back in. "Am I in danger?" she squeaked.

"Of course not!" he lied again, shoving her. Artemis wasn't a picture of strength, but the contact shocked her enough that she lost her footing. He slammed the door as she took a tumble down the steps, landing hard on her hip. I automatically bent to brush dirt off her; she shuddered at the touch of my invisible hands, climbed to her feet and fled.

Chapter 7

The boys gathered at sunset.

The place they chose for the ritual was just off the Old Quarry Trail, which was in the daytime a popular and well-marked route for suburban hikers. Teachers often found reasons to take classes there on nature walks, so my friends knew the trail well. About midway through the shortest loop, past the marsh bridge and just over a hill, was a large clearing over which the final sliver of moon shone brightly. They set up on the flattest patch of grass.

They drew a series of interlocked circles in salt, with the hair and teeth they'd collected placed in the spaces where the lines intersected. The fetal pig, still defrosting from a week in Jackson's deep freeze, marked the centre. (The cauldron remained with the rest of the pots and pans in Brady's mother's kitchen, an unnecessary impulse buy on his part).

Jackson sliced his hand with the blade of a paring knife, letting a drop fall onto the pig before dipping a finger into the wound. He winced, and so did I. *I can't believe this is actually happening.* I couldn't tell if that was my thought or his. With the book lying open at his feet, he set about replicating the sigils on the page, using his index finger to paint thick red lines on his forehead and cheeks.

Even without knowing the full consequences of failure, Jackson had been extraordinarily precise. Not content with Google Translate, he'd scoured bookstores for a Latin-to-English dictionary to ensure they got each step exactly right. He practiced the pronunciations every night after his parents went to sleep. It wouldn't be enough. They'd already made their error.

The fetus.

I'd watched enough fantasy TV shows to understand that magic demanded balance; you had to take a life to give one. And even if that weren't a hard-and-fast rule, any spell authored by Nyhiloteph would require an act of evil. They thought they could cheat the book, but they couldn't.

The thin pages rustled, though there was no breeze, and the book's spine felt suddenly clammy, like fevered flesh. A new line appeared on the page as Jackson read it, nestled between the ingredient list and the numbered steps.

"Guys?"

"What's up?" Abdul was painting Brady's forehead, blinking away the drips oozing below his brows.

"We forgot something. There's…another component that I didn't see before."

"I thought you went through everything?" Abdul asked. His wrist twitched, the brush jabbing Brady in the eye.

"Ow!"

"The ink was faded," Jackson lied. "I was barely able to make it out."

"Is it also Latin?" Brady asked.

Abdul scoffed. "Why would it not be?"

"I translated it," Jackson replied.

"You mean Google did," said Abdul.

"Fuck you, it's not like you helped."

"What does it say?" Brady cut in.

Jackson looked sheepish. "It's garbled, but it's something like 'A loved woman must be present.'"

"What does that mean?" asked Abdul.

"Could it mean Lucy?" Brady asked. "I mean, we're fond of her. That's why we're doing this."

"But she's not present," Abdul said.

Brady shrugged. "She will be."

"It's an ingredient," Jackson snapped. "The woman needs to be here when the spell is cast."

"Adrienne, then."

"Seriously, Brady."

"I'm being serious." Brady shrugged. "I mean, who else could it be? It's not like either of us are getting laid."

"Well, that settles that," Abdul said. "Can't say we didn't try."

"What are you talking about?" Jackson asked.

"I'm sure she'd come if Jack asked her," Brady added.

A coyote howled in the distance. Abdul lowered his voice, as if worried someone was listening from the trees. "You're not suggesting we ritually sacrifice someone?"

"Of course not!" Jackson exclaimed, and Brady laughed. His voice echoed across the field, before getting sucked into the brush.

"Shit, man. Did you actually think that's what it meant?"

"Neither of you have any idea what it means," Adbul shot back.

"Bingo," I said.

"Abby," Jackson reasoned, "you know I would never do that to Adrienne. Or anyone."

"I believe you," Abdul replied. "But you don't know what's going to happen when we do this spell. We could be leading Adrienne to her death if we bring her here. Frankly, this could kill all of us, but at least we knew that going in." He wiped his forehead with his sleeve, smearing the bloody designs. "I'm leaving. This isn't right."

"You can't! The book says we need three people."

"Don't try to stop me."

Jackson slumped, the hurt visible on his face. "Who do you think I am?"

"I think you're unwell right now," Abdul replied, backing away from the circle. He kept his eyes on them until he reached the tree line, at which point he took off like a shot and didn't look back. Thank fuck.

Nyhiloteph waited for Abdul's white shirt to disappear in the trees, then turned to me. "He'll regret that."

"Not if you can't get a third," I retorted.

I steeled myself for violence, recalling again the feel of his hands on me, but the demon just chortled. I looked back to the circle and saw Jackson sending a text.

Woken by the text chime, Adrienne groped for the phone on her nightstand. I knocked it out of her hand as her fingers wrapped around it. "Back to bed," I hissed.

She flicked on her lamp and rolled over to retrieve the device, running her finger across the screen to search for hairline cracks. The text popped up.

JACKSON: you up?

She unlocked the phone and typed a reply: now I am.

JACKSON: This sounds really weird but I need you to come find me.

Adrienne's muscles tensed. Did she remember the half-transmitted warning from the séance, or if did she just think this was the strangest booty call ever?

"Ignore it," I said. "Go to sleep."

Gritting her teeth, she typed: send me your location.

I tried so hard to stop Adrienne from getting there. Every step of the way, I tripped her, whipped up dirt and litter into blinding sandstorms, ripped branches from trees and threw them at her like a malevolent sprite from a fairy tale. All of it only sharpened her resolve. Something was trying to stop her from helping Jackson, and she wasn't going to let it.

Fucking typical.

Of course, once she crossed the threshold of the Old Quarry Trail, Nyhiloteph made sure every branch parted to let her through.

I couldn't stand to watch what was about to happen, so I blasted myself once again into Artemis's sleeping brain.

"You have to stop this!" I yelled in my stilted, declarative dream-voice. "This is all your fault!"

"It's not," Artemis said calmly. "It's yours."

"You sold him the book."

"And you led him to it."

I felt like he'd popped me with a pin. "You don't know that."

"You're in my head. The one-way mirror works two ways now."

"Fuck," I said. "I didn't mean to. I wanted him to buy a séance from you."

"That would have been better for both of us, yes."

"What do I do now?" I asked despairingly, hoping he'd have some sort of potion or incantation I could use to undo all that had gone wrong.

"You can handle your own business and let me get some sleep," he retorted, and a kick to the stomach sent me spiralling back into reality.

I emerged from the fake forest in Artemis' brain into the real one.

"Welcome back," Nyhiloteph said.

"Thanks," I replied, still jarred from the ejection.

"Didn't know that medium of yours had it in him."

I side-eyed the demon. "Does everyone know my business, now?"

"There's no secrets on this side. I have broken the lock on the fuzzy pink diary of your mind."

Adrienne and Jackson were arguing.

"Just humour him," Brady interrupted. "That's what I'm doing."

"It probably won't work," Jackson admitted, and Nyhiloteph chortled.

"Bullshit," Adrienne snapped. "You wouldn't be doing all this if you didn't think something would happen." She put a hand on Jackson's shoulder. "Listen, no one understands what you're going through more than I do. Sometimes I think the guilt is going to drown me, that I'll never deserve to be happy ever again. And sometimes bad things happen to me and I feel like I'm being punished. As much as I tell myself I wasn't at fault, I was the one behind the wheel, and if Lucy hates me from beyond the grave she has the right to." She blinked away tears. "But Lucy was your friend. Would she want you to punish yourself?"

"I don't!" I yelled.

"Yes," Nyhiloteph contradicted me. "She does." His voice was louder than mine, not loud enough to be heard by the living but strong enough to break into Jackson's subconscious. "Not going through with this would be like killing her all over again."

"You fucking bastard," I hissed. Nyhiloteph raised a claw to his lips, shushing me.

Jackson's voice broke. "I have to try to make this right," he said, brandishing the book as if it were an argument in itself. "Now that I know that there might be a way to bring her back, it would be like I'm killing her all over again if I don't."

"But you didn't kill her!" Adrienne yelled. "I did!"

"But what if you could take that back?" Nyhiloteph said softly. There was none of his signature force behind the question; the sound travelled at a leisurely pace, moving this way and that with the breeze. When it finally drifted into Adrienne's head, it must have felt no different than one of her own thoughts.

"Don't listen to him!" I cried, though I already knew my voice wouldn't penetrate.

She stiffened, stared into space, then locked eyes with Jackson. "What do we need to do?"

The book fell out of Jackson's hands and flew open.

The first stage of the ritual went as rehearsed. Holding hands with Adrienne and Brady, Jackson read the Latin incantation. Nyhiloteph snickered whenever his pronunciation was off. As he said the words, correctly or not, sparks formed on the offerings. The pig burst into flames first, followed by the teeth and hair; Nyhiloteph swelled as the fire consumed the items, his penis standing at attention. Once he'd absorbed what he needed, he commenced screwing around.

New instructions materialized on the pages, demanding increasingly humiliating displays of subjugation. He made the boys disrobe and rub the blasphemous ashes over their bodies, had them remove their shoes and step on the smoldering remains. Jackson despaired as he translated each passage, double checking each command before conceding that yes, they did have to swallow the unburnt teeth, snort the ashes, and anything else the demon could dream up. If any of them thought to refuse, Nyhiloteph snatched the idea from their minds.

I wanted to puke as I watched the display. Brady did several times, doubling over to spit up bile when there was no food left in his stomach. Tears streamed down his cheeks, blending with sickness sweat. Shivering on the sidelines, Adrienne seemed to shrink into herself, her squeezed-shut eyes retreating into their sockets. Jackson was hysterical, muttering manic affirmations that didn't make anyone feel any better. "We're almost done, just one more step, you're doing great, just think of something else…"

When they finally climaxed, the demon's black bug eyes went wide. His clawed hands clenched, his back arched. There was a sound like snapping fingers and he was gone.

Adrienne's head cracked backward.

Chapter 8

The snap was so loud, I thought her neck had broken. Jackson caught her as she fell to her knees, lowering her to the ground. Her eyes rolled halfway into her skull, lids fluttering.

"Ade! Are you okay?"

She didn't react as Jackson shook her, until she suddenly did, pushing him away and crawling backward on her hands and knees.

Chest heaving, Adrienne looked at Jackson, then Brady, then around her into the darkened woods, her eyes wide like a cornered animal. If she'd willingly come here, she didn't remember that now. She looked at her hands, gaping at the alien appendages. "Where am I?" It was my voice that came from her lips. Of course, it wasn't me.

Part II:

Dead Ringer

Chapter 9

"You want the front seat, Lucy?"

Through the rear-view mirror, Nyhiloteph glared from Adrienne's eyes. "Not after what happened last time."

"Fair," Jackson mumbled, and reversed out of the laneway. His face was ashen beneath the ritual grime, and his voice came out strangled in his attempt to sound casual. He was trying to keep himself together for what he believed was my benefit, but it was Adrienne's name that was bouncing around his skull. At one point he was about to ask if she was still in there somewhere, but another glance at the face in the mirror made him reconsider. A tomorrow problem.

"Listen, I know this is totally my fault-"

"You think?" the Nyhiloteph/Adrienne hybrid snapped, the culmination of a twenty-minute car ride of angry sulking. I willed Jackson to see through the charade. Surely he couldn't believe the hostile spirit in Adrienne's body was me.

"Do you want to talk?" he asked.

"No, Jackson. I just want to go home." Nyhiloteph hitched with a sob. "Fuck, I can't even go to my home. I have to go to

Adrienne's..." The sob eased into a gentle weeping. Even I had to admit it was a nice touch.

Jackson left Nyhiloteph at the end of Adrienne's driveway, asking, "Are you sure?" before driving off. Nyhiloteph waved and watched the car disappear around the corner, rubbing the gooseflesh on his new arms. He studied the house, on alert for the flicking of a light or the parting of a curtain, then turned and started walking.

Headed towards the lane of lost dreams.

Chapter 10

Artemis was at the Grimoire when Nyhiloteph knocked on the door. The medium jumped, then slouched deeper behind the stack of books, one eye protruding to watch the entrance. The outline of a young woman formed in the frosted glass.

He couldn't have gotten up if he'd wanted to. The door opened anyway, chain lock scraping and falling, knob turning without her having to touch it.

"Old friend," the demon said, in the sweet, high voice of Adrienne. "Burning the midnight oil?"

Artemis stood, walking around the front of the desk and falling to his knees. "The penultimate conversion is complete," he stammered. "Congratulations, your honour."

"No thanks to you."

"The ghost girl asked me for help," he protested, forehead touching the floorboards. "I turned her down."

"Yes," Nyhiloteph said, flipping his blonde hair. "But out of fear, more than love."

"Isn't it safer to be feared than loved?"

Nyhiloteph shrugged, examining the spine of a rare book before throwing it to the floor. "Some would say so. I was never that Machiavellian. But while we're on the subject - what you have there?"

"Just inventory."

Nyhiloteph raised a hand. The book at the bottom of the biggest pile removed itself, unsettling all the others, and flew into his palm. "Ad Mortem. My Latin's a little fuzzy, but doesn't that mean, Back to Death?" He raised an eyebrow. It was perfectly plucked and pencilled, a stark contrast to the ash smeared across Adrienne's face.

"Do you know what kind of store this is? Every book in here is like that."

The demon's voice shifted, abandoning Adrienne's soft inflection in favour of his own deep, cavernous tone. "This wasn't on your desk when the girl came in today. Neither were all the others. I can read the spines from here. Summonings and Reversals by Damien LaForge? Binding the Spirits, by that hack pretender to the knighthood, Sir Andrew Scott? I wonder why you saw fit to take them out, tonight of all nights."

Artemis opened his mouth but Nyhiloteph cut him off, shifting back into his girl's voice - which retained an oddly hollow note, like the echo of laughter in an abyss. "I'm bored of you."

"Then, leave," the medium snapped.

"Wouldn't that be nice."

"Honestly!" Artemis cried, defiance drained from his tone. "You'll never have to deal with me again if you just leave me alone.

There's nothing I can do to stop you, I know that. Yeah, I looked up some counter-spells, but that was just insur-"

The words died on his lips as his head slammed into the floor. Twice his face smashed against the wood, hard, and then his shoulders rose, like a marionette on a string. The medium's throat was white and blotchy, constricted by an invisible hand. He was upright just long enough for me to see the broken nose and shattered teeth, gums gushing blood. His chin looked misshapen, bent in a different direction. Then he was brought down again, neck snapping with the force. I think he might have died at that point, but the demon continued to bash his face in until there was none of it left.

I couldn't watch. Behind me, Adrienne was swaying limply, teeth chattering. Nyhiloteph had left her body for the moment, but she was too numbed with terror to escape. I rushed to her side with vague, panicked thoughts of doing something, but Nyhiloteph slammed back into her before I could. He cocked her head and raised her right hand. I recoiled, fearing he was about to hit me, if that were even possible.

But no blow came. He let me watch as he waggled Adrienne's fingers, a gesture I didn't understand until he spoke. "Prints," he said, the voice an unholy hybrid of his own and his host's. "No fingerprints now, but I could really mess up her life if I added some."

"Why would you want to do that?" I asked. "You have to live as her."

Nyhiloteph knew I was there, but couldn't hear me from her body. He kept talking anyway. "Then again, your police don't like to send pretty blonde girls to prison. I think they'd offer her a plea deal if we said it was Jackson who dragged her here. Any of them, really, but the boyfriend makes the most sense."

Nyhiloteph strolled towards Artemis' lifeless body, knocking books off the shelves as he went. He let Adrienne's splayed fingers hover over the corpse's throat – then, just as they were about to touch down, he snatched the hand away. "Maybe later," Nyhiloteph laughed, voice girlish. "Wouldn't want to miss out on grad."

Chapter 11

Melodramatically naming things runs in my family, and I deemed the next morning The Day of Sobs. Artemis's post-mortem anguish was so great it permeated the atmosphere, the weeping on the air so loud I could hear nothing else. It took me hours to locate his spirit, crumpled in the Grimoire's crawlspace, ruined face cradled in his arms.

I've never been the most comforting person, but it helped that I could sense the misery radiating off him in all its gradations. I knew what he was feeling to an extent, most dominantly guilt and shame. That was one thing Nyhiloteph had been right about - there were few secrets among the dead.

"Hey," I said, sitting next to him along the slanted ceiling, hoping my voice sounded soothing. "So, this sucks."

When he raised his head, the stench of viscera and rotting flesh hit me.

"You know, you don't have to...exist like that," I said.

"Expert of the afterlife, now?"

I was actually shocked he could speak, considering how fucked his mouth was.

I shrugged. "I've been here longer."

He groaned - an exasperated groan, not the ghost-y, chain-rattling kind. "I devoted my whole life to the mysteries of the world beyond."

"And now here you are, lowest rung on the ladder. Death really is the great leveller."

"This is your fault, you know."

"Don't throw stones. I don't blame you for the not-stopping-Nyhiloteph thing. I'm also scared shitless of the guy. But if you had been able to summon fucking Warren, or whatever his name was, instead of just grabbing me, none of us would be in this situation."

I felt him shrivel with remorse, overcome with the belief that he was being punished, doomed by his cowardice to an afterlife of mutilation and pain. He hid his ruined face in his hands again.

"Favourite song," I blurted out.

"What?"

"If you want to exist as more than the moment of your death, you have to re-connect with who you were in life," I explained. "Quickly, preferably. What...is...your...favourite...song?"

He thought for a second, looked ready to reject the exercise as stupid. The song was probably embarrassing, I guessed, but refused to give him an out.

"Dead Ringer for Love."

"Never heard it."

"Meat Loaf. Cher sang on it."

"I only know him from Rocky Horror," I admitted. "Can you sing it?"

"Fuck, no."

"Do you have a copy we can play here?"

"I've got a record player."

"That works."

I led him through the ceiling and out of the crawlspace, hoping he would brighten in the familiarity of his store. But I'd forgotten the damage wreaked by Nyhiloteph – shelves knocked down, books thrown around and bent out of shape, the face-shaped pool of blood and the Artemis-shaped corpse in the middle of it all.

"Record player!" I snapped, sensing his resolve wither. I wondered if the wispy, incomprehensible ghosts people see in inhospitable places are just spirits like Artemis who never had anyone to nudge them out of the attic.

He ushered me into the séance room, where he lifted a flap of tablecloth to reveal a milk crate full of vinyl. "They had to change the size of these," he muttered. "People were stealing them."

"Records?"

"Milk crates."

The collection was in alphabetical order, but *Dead Ringer* was at the front of the stack. "Player and speakers are by my desk."

I took the record from him and examined its comic book-style cover, the muscled man whisking a bevy of beautiful women through a churning, otherworldly sea. Artemis watched me admire it, a collector showing off. He was starting to look better even now.

His face was bending back into shape, and the blood was beginning to dry and flake.

His turntable was set up behind the cash. "What were you saying about the milk crates?"

"The old ones used to be the exact width of a vinyl record. They had to start making them slightly smaller because people were stealing them from grocery stores."

"And then the CD was invented and crime dropped 80%."

He gave me a look.

"How does it work?"

Artemis lifted the lid and gestured for me to hand back the album. Gingerly removing the record, edges held between the tips of his fingers, he placed it on the turntable and manipulated the needle. "If that's the song you want," he said, as if I'd picked the song, "we have to drop the needle about here." He pressed PLAY and the record started to spin.

The needle caught the tail end of a spoken word piece, then a grandiose guitar riff slashed the silence. A saxophone wail, then pianos and power chords pounding in tandem. They formed an overcrowded backdrop to Meat Loaf's anguished voice, singing about a dive bar one-night stand as if it were a love story for the ages. Cher entered on the second verse, matching his intensity note-for-note. He was Eddie, she was his Magenta, and this was "Whatever Happened to Saturday Night?" on cocaine.

I was so taken by the song I'd forgotten to pay attention to Artemis. I turned from the record player toward a phantasmagorical vision.

A massive, throbbing jukebox had materialized in the bookstore, casting pink and green neon across the floorboards. Next to it was a young man in a leather jacket, jeans ripped at the knees, combat boots scuffed. Shaggy brown hair hung over his eyes; the rest of his face was obscured by the weird shadows of the jukebox lights. He was dancing like an old rock-n-roller, hand extended to dip and spin an unseen partner. He laughed at something I couldn't hear, his mouth opening wide to expose a set of crooked teeth. This was the medium, distilled to his purest dreams, what he'd always felt like or hoped to be. What he'd never be, except in this fleeting moment.

The song ended too soon, dimming the glow of the jukebox and plunging the room into darkness. By the time my eyes adjusted, the jukebox was gone, as was the greaser. Artemis was sitting cross-legged on the floor just a few feet from his body, his face intact, lips moving as he sang along to the final power ballad.

Chapter 12

Nyhiloteph slept all morning, like a beast after a feeding. Adrienne's parents knocked at ten and eleven, but he screamed until they left. He could get away with that; everyone knew Adrienne was going through a hard time. At one o'clock, a rock clattered against the window. Peeling blood-caked hair out of his eyes, Nyhiloteph rose to find Jackson on the lawn.

"Can I come up?" he whisper-yelled.

Switching to my voice, Nyhiloteph called back, "Knock on the door, dumbass. Adrienne's parents'll let you in."

Nyhiloteph examined himself in the mirror, liking the way his blonde waves and sparkling blue eyes offset the brown-black clumps and ashy smears, the way the dried blood on his new hands contrasted garishly with his pink-painted nails. On the first floor Jackson fumbled his way past the de Keysers, introducing himself awkwardly. "Come in," Nyhiloteph cooed.

He was standing in the doorway when Jackson reached the top of the stairs, arms stretched high above his head to grab either side of the frame. Jackson lurched to such a stop that I thought he was going to fall right back down.

"What?" Nyhiloteph asked. "You expected me to pretty myself up?"

"I just forgot…"

I kept waiting for him to put the dots together, to notice there was more blood on Adrienne now than when he dropped her off.

"Are you mad that I'm not taking proper care of her?" the demon taunted. "Don't play dumb. I saw what you and Adrienne were getting up to when I was in the ground."

I rolled my eyes. Jackson and I had never been together, not even close, so why would I care if he had a girlfriend? It was good that Nyhiloteph didn't know that, though; his jealous ex act would raise suspicion.

"She's very nice," Jackson protested.

Nyhiloteph raised an eyebrow. "Present tense? You're sure she still exists?"

I wanted to know that, too.

Jackson looked at his shoes. "I was thinking…you should probably learn some things about Adrienne so you can…pass as her. Until we get this figured out."

"Kinky," Nyhiloteph said. "Do tell."

"Don't you dare," I said, and I almost thought Jackson heard me, because the next thing he said was: "Don't you want to…take a shower, or something?"

Nyhiloteph raised a finger to his lips, chewing on a nail. "What, you wanna watch?" Jackson blanched.

Adrienne's bedroom had its own full bath, and Nyhiloteph made Jackson wait as he showered and washed Adrienne's hair. Jackson leaned against the wall, his eyes not leaving the bathroom door. I wondered how much of his power of persuasion Nyhiloteph had retained post-possession. Why else would

Jackson immediately start scheming to help Nyhiloteph - or me, in his mind - pass as Adrienne? Didn't he want her back?

The demon came out naked, scrubbed and shiny, Adrienne's blonde curls wrapped half-assedly in a towel. "You've seen this already," Nyhiloteph pointed out when Jackson averted his eyes.

"Not quite in the same context."

"True."

Nyhiloteph slipped back into Adrienne's bed and wrapped himself in her sheets, unconcerned with the bloody handprint.

"Jackson?" he asked, in the gentlest tone he could manage in my voice.

"What?"

"Seriously, how are you doing? I know you've been going through a really hard time and, well, I guess this made everything worse."

Jackson shrugged. "It's my fault," he said, aiming for nonchalance and not quite getting there. "It's all my fault."

Nyhiloteph patted the bed and Jackson collapsed into his arms. I bristled, second-hand embarrassment as much as anger. I'd never been a hugger.

An odour filled the room, the thick, sickly scent of lavender. Clean flesh, freshly washed hair, and floral deodorant: Adrienne's smell. Nyhiloteph's soft hands moved up Jackson's arms, back, and shoulders, massaging the stress out of his joints. I saw the demon's mouth open, heard the little intake of the lungs that culminated in an exhale of Adrienne's breath, its scent evoking intimate moments, flaring hormones and arousal. Losing himself in the space between a sob, Jackson pressed his lips to Nyhiloteph's.

The edge of the demon's mouth flitted upward as he opened his eyes. Almost like he was looking right at me.

Nyhiloteph let the kiss linger for about five seconds before pushing Jackson off. He rolled off the bed and onto his feet, one hand touching his lips as if restraining them from a fight, the other covering his bulging crotch.

"Lucy, I'm so sorry, I-"

"Forgot I was gay?" I asked.

He'd never really gotten that through his head. But we'd never really discussed our romantic lives, aside from my impulsive, awkward coming-out that ended with me exclaiming, "sorry for the info-dump!" So we were both sexual non-entities, as far as the other was concerned.

"It's okay," Nyhiloteph said, pulling the blankets to his chest. "I guess it was like, muscle memory?"

I found myself nodding along with Jackson. He'd forgotten I wasn't Adrienne. It was understandable. Weird, but understandable. And he was bewitched.

Nyhiloteph giggled, which I'd never seen him do before without cruelty. "You've become such a stud since I left."

Jackson started to giggle, a mix of horror and relief, and then they were both shaking with mirth, laughter as alternative to screaming. They looked like a pair of old friends. I had to restrain myself from breaking a mirror or shaking a lamp.

Nyhiloteph wiped moisture from his eyes. "We should attend to the task at hand," he announced, an echo of a laugh still in his voice - my voice. "Tell me about your girlfriend.

Adrienne's favourite band was The Killers. Her dog was a Maltese named Pillow and she was the only one in the family who let it sleep in her bed. Her right eye twitched when she was tired, and she had a weird habit of blurting out non-sequiturs that turned out to be half-remembered reality show quotes a given situation reminded her of. She turned movies off when an animal died.

Every new fact, every confirmation of her humanity, twisted the knife in my gut. Eventually I couldn't take it anymore and transferred back to The Grimoire. I was in a mood, so I clicked on the record player and turned up the speaker.

"That's a little loud," Artemis warned from behind his desk, as Liz Phair filled the room.

"Did your best guy friend ever try to make out with you?"

"Unfortunately, no." He remained fixed on an old book, tracing words with his finger. "Seriously, be careful with that," he added. "We don't need a noise complaint sending cops to my door."

I glanced at where his body lay, buzzing with flies. I couldn't smell the corpse, though the reek of Artemis's wounds had been clear to me in their ghostly form. Its sound was more prominent, though the vibrations of the insects were white noise by now. There would be maggots soon.

"How much time do you think we have?" I asked. "Speaking of…that."

He shrugged, still flipping pages. "That CLOSED sign is doing a lot of work."

"We won't get evicted once you stop paying the bills?"

"The building's mine, utilities are direct deposit."

"Expecting any visitors? Friends or family?"

He gave me a look.

"So, all we have to worry about is Nyhiloteph showing up to fuck shit up?" I concluded.

"Which is a possibility."

"Why hasn't he?" I asked, turning the volume down. "Surely he knows we're here."

"Maybe not," Artemis replied. "I think he's limited when he's in that body. He can't see as widely as he used to, can't travel the same way we can because he's tied to the flesh. He had to vacate it to kill me."

I remembered how Adrienne had stood by as Nyhiloteph's invisible claws grabbed and battered Artemis. "She looked so empty."

"That's generally how it goes."

"Where do you think she is?"

Artemis ignored me for a second, squinting to decipher smudge of word-shaped ink. "Dunno. I wouldn't count on her being much help."

"Is there any way we can get Nyhiloteph out of her?"

Artemis sat up, fixed me with an exasperated glare, and held up the book he was reading. It was an instruction guide for Catholic exorcisms.

"Oh," I said. "Gotcha."

65

Chapter 13

Nyhiloteph stood in front of Adrienne's closet, making sense of the crush of outfits. Like everything under Adrienne's control, it was meticulously organized: skirts and shorts, arranged by length, dangling from clip hangers, a rainbow of tank tops and t-shirts, and finally a week's worth of brightly-coloured sundresses. (Her jeans and winter clothes were folded neatly in drawers, colour-coded because of course they were).

Clothes landed in heaps on the floor as Nyhiloteph swatted the hangers from side to side, searching for a perfect item that Adrienne didn't own. The demon finally settled on Adrienne's darkest and skimpiest outfit – a black halter top paired with distressed jean shorts. After applying make-up – a dramatic smoky eye that looked way out of character for his host - he descended the stairs to find Adrienne's mother making breakfast. "You're not wearing that to school, are you?" she asked.

"Are you gonna stop me?" Nyhiloteph growled.

He left without eating.

Abdul watched Nyhiloteph struggle with Adrienne's locker. "I don't know," he said. "She just looks like Adrienne to me."

"Nah, man," Brady insisted. "You weren't there. It was Lucy." He nudged Abdul forward. "You're it! Go get her."

"You're not coming?"

Brady shook his head. "You two have some shit to work out. Me, she's cool with." He was halfway down the hall in the other direction before Abdul had a chance to protest.

Nyhiloteph was swearing under his breath, which perhaps did remind Abdul of me. The fact that he didn't know Adrienne's combination also tracked. Still, if Brady had been bullshitting – which was also like Brady – Abdul would be approaching the most popular girl in school, babbling nonsensically.

"Hey," he whispered, looking around to see if there was anyone else he could presumably be talking to.

"If it isn't the person who wanted to leave me for dead," Nyhiloteph replied, keeping his back to him.

Abdul's mind split in two directions, his first instinct being to correct the idiom; you can't leave someone for dead if they're long-dead already. Then he gasped, recognizing my voice. "It's really you."

"Dead to you."

"I'm so sorry. I honestly didn't understand what was going on, I freaked out..."

Nyhiloteph twisted the lock and slammed open the door, its edge denting the locker adjacent. "I guess in a crisis, you learn who your real friends are."

Abdul's face crumpled, and Nyhiloteph spread his arms. "Kidding. Hug it out?"

Watching Abdul of all people embrace someone he believed to be me was the weirdest fucking thing I'd ever seen. Abdul was even more of a non-hugger than I was. I wondered why Nyhiloteph was so touchy-feely, then I remembered his demonic erection in Jackson's bedroom with Adrienne, and his advances on Jackson afterward. This was just a platonic hug, but it was a violation, wasn't it? Demanding intimacy he didn't deserve, pretending to be someone he wasn't.

Nyhiloteph released him with a rib-crushing squeeze. "This will take adjusting to," he said, gesturing at his new body. "But at least the gang's back together."

"Wait, you want things to stay this way?" Abdul blurted out.

Nyhiloteph let Adrienne's face fall. "Of course," he said. "What else would I want?"

"But…" Abdul stammered, "…but it isn't your body."

"It is now."

"But what about Adrienne?"

"Why the fuck do you care about Adrienne?"

"Well…"

"Seriously, I can see why Jackson's hung up – he was fucking her."

Abdul shrunk. "It's not about Adrienne, per se. It's just…it's her body. It's not right."

Nyhiloteph glared with such force I thought Abdul was going to melt in its heat. "Was it right when that bitch, who shouldn't have been driving in the first place, ran a red and sent three thousand pounds of metal careening into me? Just me, of course. You guys all walked away with a cool story. I lost everything."

"But she doesn't deserve to die."

"And I did? Listen, I don't know what you guys did to get me back, and I guess things got hairy out in the woods there, but don't you think it worked out?" Abdul didn't answer. The demon pushed. "If you ask me, this put everything right. Well, not everything, but pretty close. If one of us has to be dead, it makes sense that it's her and not me."

"I guess," Abdul conceded.

Nyhiloteph placed his hand on Abdul's shoulder. "Don't second guess a miracle."

Chapter 14

Adrienne had been a conscientious planner, and the demon slipped seamlessly into her life. Adhering to the schedule mapped out in her pink Moleskine agenda, he showed up on time, made the customary small talk, and sat quietly in class, filing his nails into sharp points.

Vocally, he imitated Adrienne perfectly; only when alone with the guys did he slip back into my voice. In mixed company, he landed somewhere in between; it sounded exactly like I would if I were trying to impersonate her; just good enough to pass for Adrienne, just off enough so my friends still heard me underneath.

I was curious to hear what people would say about him when he wasn't there, but refused to leave the demon unattended. All his good behaviour only made me more suspicious.

The Grad Oscars committee met during their spare period, in a vacant classroom reserved for the Drama program. Half-dressed mannequins and deconstructed sets from the year's production of *Sweeney Todd* leaned against the walls, adding an aura of Victorian grimness. The four committee members – Adrienne, Michelle Myers, Nalo Richardson, and Kerri Light - sat in a circle in the centre of the room, notebooks in their laps, spreadsheets open on smartphones.

The awards results were rigged – the girls had collected the student votes, and were now discussing whether they agreed with the results. To my great annoyance they appointed lacrosse team jackass Carter Daniels as Class Clown, even though the votes had clearly gone for Brady. Not thinking, I jumped to my feet in protest, and the girls turned in my direction when the desk I'd been perched on jiggled. I winced, irrationally worried I'd given my position away, but no one made any remark.

Michelle Myers, the head of the committee, popped a grape into her mouth. "So for the tribute to Lucy Steinberg, we were initially just going to give her an honorary Oscar, but now that we have some nice photos of her, we'll be able to do something a little more formal. So, yayyy." She clapped softly. "Thanks, Adrienne, for getting that together."

"You should thank Jackson for that," Nyhiloteph said, arms crossed. I hated that I agreed with him.

"For sure!" Michelle replied, and after an awkward pause, added, "You don't think he'd want to deliver the tribute?"

"Probably not," Nyhiloteph said. "The boy's a charisma vacuum. I thought I would."

The atmosphere in the room seemed to curdle.

Michelle went white. "I...I'm not..."

"Lucy and I have a special relationship, don't you think?" Nyhiloteph was still doing his pitch-perfect vocal performance, but everything else was off: the mannerisms, the slouched posture and sadistic smirk, the acid dripping off his tongue. "Forever bound by fate."

Nalo chimed in. "I think that might come off as, umm, not the most sensitive? No offence."

The demon-girl's eyes widened. "You don't think people still think I killed her, do you? The police investigated – I'm cool."

Michelle's front teeth came together like a castle gate.

"Michelle's the emcee," Kerri pointed out.

"But she didn't like Lucy," Nyhiloteph argued. "None of you did. You all thought she was a loser, if you thought of her at all. And she didn't think all that highly of you."

I don't know how he knew that, but it was true; maybe he really had read through my fuzzy diary.

As if he'd read my mind, Nyhiloteph continued. "Lucy hated how Michelle made fun of Abdul and Jackson when they had law class together. And when Carter Daniels used to grope Lucy in math class, Nalo and Kerri would egg him on. Kerri, didn't you used to give him suggestions of dirty things he could whisper in her ear?"

Kerri winced. "We were kidding."

"Is that why Carter got suspended for sexual harassment? Even after you both lied to the principal and said that Carter just had a crush on her? Don't think Lucy didn't know that. She heard you bitches cackling about it afterward." Nyhiloteph's voice twisted, and suddenly he was channelling the girls: "'Like Carter would never go for such a cow.' 'I can't believe she'd complain, it's the only attention she'll ever get from a guy.'"

The girls' eyes were agape; he sounded exactly like Kerri. Surely they saw there was something unnatural about it? But this wasn't a horror movie – no one jumps right to 'demonic possession' the second someone starts acting weird.

"She used to write poems about you, you know? Comparing you to vultures. Fantasizing about luring you into the basement and walling you in. Just a literary allusion, don't worry. She'd always shred them afterward, because they made her feel like a bad person."

Nyhiloteph stood up, dropping Adrienne's agenda back into her purse. "Maybe I did kill that nerd," he concluded. "Maybe I did her a favour by putting her out of the misery you made for her. But what my actions lacked was a little thing called intent. You, on the other hand, intended to make Lucy Steinberg's life miserable. If she'd have painted the bathtub with her wrists, you'd all be morally culpable. Although no jury would convict." The bell rang, signalling an end to lunch, and he headed out the door.

I was dumbfounded. I felt like he'd stripped me naked and ripped the flesh from my bones. The Grad Oscars girls looked like they were all about to cry.

I'll never admit this to anyone, but I kind of wanted to cheer.

Michelle followed Nyhiloteph out, grabbing his arm. He shocked her by grabbing back, raking sharpened fingernails down her arm.

Michelle pulled free. "You freak!"

"You don't know the half of it," Nyhiloteph replied, baring his teeth. Reflected in Michelle's eyes, they looked for a moment like jagged fangs, but when she blinked they were just Adrienne's teeth, straight and precise from two years of braces. She turned away, rubbing the angry wound on her arm. She was heading back into the drama room to inform the girls of Adrienne's latest outrage (She must have hit her head in that car crash) when she abruptly halted. "Adrienne?"

Nyhiloteph was walking slowly. "Yes?"

Michelle's voice was robotic. "On second thought, it is probably best if you do the tribute. She means so much to you."

"I'm glad you've come around," Nyhiloteph said, in a voice that made my legs wobble. It was his true voice, the old and impossibly deep one I'd heard in the bookstore. I wondered how he dared. Then he was Adrienne again, flipping his hair and grinning like a pageant queen. "I'll leave you to inform the Committee."

Chapter 15

"I didn't know you smoked, Adrienne."

Nyhiloteph was blowing elaborate rings in the smoker's pit, a little patch of anarchy where the stoners, rockers, and skaters came to skip class. Today's assembly was an amiable mix of 21st century hippies, Hot Topic mall goths, and punks who might have time travelled from the '70s, hair dyed and gelled, decked with piercings and Clash patches.

A cheer erupted from the edge of the crowd, and a tenth grader with a foot-high yellow mohawk called out, "Look who they let out!" The pit parted to admit a tall punk with scraggly red hair, denim jacket jangling with chains.

"I thought they'd thrown away the key on you," Brady laughed. The newcomer shoved Brady before wrapping him in a one-armed hug. "Justin here was a political prisoner," Brady explained. When Nyhiloteph squinted quizzically, he added, "Principal's office."

Nyhiloteph chortled, sucking down the smoke like it was oxygen. "What were you in for?"

Justin put on an aw, shucks grin. "Marsters caught me tearing down a bunch of posters for the Washington trip."

"To what end?"

The vandal shrugged. "I just don't think we should be spending our money there. It's Wall Street."

"I think Wall Street is in New York."

Justin paused. "And I didn't support that trip either."

"That was the band trip," corrected an orange-haired girl with a choker. "They wouldn't let you join the band."

"The school band?" Nyhiloteph asked. "I thought they let everyone in."

"Nahh," Justin said. "I tried to sign up in grade nine; Mr. Jones took one look at me and said, 'I'm not sure we're your speed, son, we don't play any Sex Pistols.' Asshole."

"That's awful," Nyhiloteph said.

"Nahh," Justin replied. "I just wanted the credit. Hey, anyone got a light?"

Nyhiloteph handed him a Bic, accidentally-on-purpose brushing the back of Justin's hand with Adrienne's manicured fingers.

Chapter 16

Adrienne's planner had her attending that day's basketball game, which is where I drew the line. Even the spectacle of the demon muttering under his breath whenever our players went to shoot, making shot after shot bounce off the rim, couldn't peak my interest in sports.

Back at the Grimoire, Artemis was still scouring every book he owned ("every legitimate book," he corrected) in search of a solution. He listened to music while he read, so the shelves rattled with the reverberations of David Bowie's "Watch That Man." He worked standing up, occasionally dipping his nose close to the page, his foot tapping in time with the glam beat. I wondered if he'd liked dancing in life. Like every other question I had about Artemis, I didn't ask it. He had a firewall around his past, and the last thing I needed was for him to flee back into the attic.

Still, I was bored, and desperate for conversation, so I turned to what I assumed would be a safe subject. "How did you end up with all these records?" I queried, assuming he'd either inform me that they sell vinyl records in many major retail outlets, or regale me with tales of thrift stores and flea markets. I didn't know which would be less engrossing.

His actual answer surprised me. "Inherited them, same as the store."

"You inherited the store? From who?"

"A fortune teller named Madame Jade."

I thought he was fucking with me. "Seriously?"

"I do not lie."

"I've seen you lie," I retorted. "How did you meet this fortune teller?"

He sighed. "I was seventeen and...between homes. Don't ask. Anyway, I was doing that thing where you walk around looking for work, offering to mow lawns and do odd jobs, and I knocked on the door here. Jade took one look at me and could tell everything about my life. She knew my parents had kicked me out and why. She said she sensed immense power in me that I might not be aware of yet. I thought she was scamming me into paying for a palm reading or something, but instead she offered me a job. Minimum wage and room and board."

The image was clear in my head. Artemis, seventeen and gangly with an even worse haircut, facing down this woman, gnarled and weathered and smelling of smoke, but with soft eyes and gentle hands. Taking his palm in hers and turning it over, tracing his lifelines with her finger and telling him his own story; his scowl that dropped and eyes that widened as she got every detail correct.

"It was the same type of store? Seances and all that?"

He nodded. "She taught me how to read fortunes and contact the dead. I thought it was just something to make money. I was a kid, everything was about money for me. After she died, I knew better."

"Did you talk to her?" I asked. "I mean, after…"

"Never could. That was when I started reading everything she'd left behind – the real books, I mean. Let's be honest, most of the stuff we stock is shit – pop occultism for goths and horror freaks." He shrugged. "Madame Jade was a capitalist."

"She was legit, though?"

"As much as any of us are," he snapped. "It's not a science."

"I can tell."

"Fuck off."

Even now, his attention remained fixed on the book, his index finger travelling steadily down the page, hitting bottom as he told me off. The paper crinkled. Artemis yelped.

I hopped up. "What?"

Steadying himself on his desk, Artemis held up the book for me. "I believe I've figured out what type of demon our friend is."

Some sort of old-timey occult encyclopedia, each page displayed crude pencil illustrations alongside long paragraphs of text, so smudged I didn't understand how Artemis could make any sense of it. He pointed to the bottom of the second page. "Look familiar?"

The drawing was hardly more than a sketch, as if the artist barely dared to depict his subject. It was a fat, hunched thing covered in spiky fur; between its legs a long phallus extended, culminating in what looked like open mouth of a snake, fangs too large for its maw. That last element may have been dramatic

license - but otherwise, the drawing looked exactly like Nyhiloteph.

81

Chapter 17

Nyhiloteph fixed his make-up from the bleachers, Adrienne's silver compact catching light from the fluorescents, flashing into players' eyes to cause a trip-and-fall pile-up. When a referee started stalking toward the stands, Nyhiloteph clicked it shut and switched it for Adrienne's planner. The game was listed in orange gel under today's date. Tomorrow's class schedule alternated pink and purple; the weekend was blank.

"I'm starving," the demon whined.

Next to him, Jackson was absorbed in his International Business textbook. "We could relocate to the Tim Hortons," he suggested, unopposed to missing the rest of the game. "I was thinking we should sit down with the guys to discuss next steps."

"Do you always talk like a corporate bootlicker?" Nyhiloteph replied, bare legs swinging in the gap between the benches.

Jackson looked hurt but chewed his lip rather than say anything.

"You're letting him have the last word?" I chided. Jackson would have debated me into submission if I'd said something like that.

"I'm craving meat," Nyhiloteph declared.

Mangled beyond recognition, the dissected cheeseburger lay prone on the silver napkin, its pleas and promises having fallen on deaf ears. Nyhiloteph scowled at it. "Is it too much to ask for a little blood on the wrapper?"

Facing Abdul, Brady mouthed the word "zombie" and was met with a glare.

"It's actually illegal in Canada to serve burgers anything less than well-done," Abdul pointed out. "Most provincial health regulations require ground beef to be cooked to 71 degrees Celsius..."

"I heard it's not actually real meat," Brady added. "My cousin said all these fast food places have been secretly using a blend of synthetic materials with like, beef DNA."

"Do you hear yourself?" Abdul asked.

Processed cheese was wedged beneath Adrienne's pink fingernail as Nyhiloteph scraped it from the patty. "So, Jackson," he announced, tone businesslike. "You said you wanted to discuss next steps?"

Abdul and Brady examined him skeptically. Jackson gaped. "Uhh..."

"Come on, I can't do all the work. I didn't come back from the dead just to carry you on another group project." This was a bastardization of that corny joke: the one about asking slacking classmates to be pallbearers. It didn't make sense in this context; neither Jackson nor Abdul had ever let anyone else take the lead on an assignment.

He chewed without pleasure before spitting the masticated hunk back into the wrapper. "I'll have Adrienne's friends out of the picture soon."

Jackson dropped his cup in his lap, was wiping root beer from his crotch even as he stared into the demon's distracted eyes. "What?"

Nyhiloteph shrugged, like what he'd said was unremarkable. There being no witnesses around, he spoke in my voice. "I've been doing an okay job of blending in so far, but I'll fuck up eventually if I spend too much time with people who knew her well."

"What are you saying?" I whispered. Was he exclusively talking about Adrienne's friends, or foreshadowing a purge of mine, too?

"I guess that makes sense," Jackson replied, blotting his spill with a napkin. "Might be good to create some *natural* distance." An awkward pause in mid-sentence, subtle emphasis on natural.

Abdul averted his eyes, pretending to read the nutrition facts on the fry packet.

"Don't go too far, though," Brady said, jocularity tempered by worry. "I mean, you don't want to make things weird for Adrienne once we put her back."

Silence. Jackson bore a guilty expression; Abdul's reticence was something else.

"We are figuring out how to do that, right?" Brady pressed, forcing a laugh.

"Of course," Nyhiloteph said, and I saw Abdul's eyes flick up, questioning the shift in rhetoric. Nyhiloteph noticed and flashed him a tight smile. That could have meant anything, but was most likely a warning.

Chapter 18

It was nearly four a.m. by the time Nyhiloteph returned to the de Keyser residence. That was a normal time for a Lucy hangout to end – my parents thought nothing of me and the guys driving around arguing about nerd stuff into the early hours– but astoundingly late for Adrienne. Nyhiloteph came home to find the lights still on, Adrienne's mother sitting in a rocking chair, eagle eyes trained on the door.

"Where the hell were you?" Eleanor demanded.

"Out," Nyhiloteph said, with a roll of his teenage eyes.

She stood up. "You don't answer your phone?"

"Not after ten p.m." The demon bypassed Eleanor to head for the kitchen. Eleanor followed her.

"And who exactly were you out with, until three-forty-five in the morning?"

"If you have to know," Nyhiloteph said, not facing her, "I was with Jackson Henderson, Abdul Al Habib, and Brady Thomas, letting each of them stick their schlong in a different orifice."

"EXCUSE ME!" Eleanor reached out to touch her daughter's shoulder. "Why are you acting like this?"

Nyhiloteph whirled around slapped her hand away. "Keep your hands off me, bitch," he hissed.

"Adie!"

Mark's bleary voice called down from upstairs. "Girls, stop fighting."

"We're not fighting," Eleanor snapped.

Nyhiloteph pushed past her to the fridge, rifling through the meat drawer for a thawing steak. Eleanor saw it on the counter when the knife drawer rattled. "What are you doing?"

"Eating," Nyhiloteph snapped. He selected a sharp-edged carving knife, rotating it to watch the gleam move along the blade.

"That's for dinner tomorrow!" Eleanor snatched the steak from the counter; Nyhiloteph jabbed the knife into her throat.

Eleanor staggered back, mouth gaping, hands grabbing at the gushing wound. She tried to scream but couldn't, her voice box punctured. Stiff-necked and clutching her throat, chin pointed upward, she looked like one of those swan-shaped fountains, blood spurting out instead of water.

An upstairs light clicked on, and Mark appeared on the landing. Nyhiloteph put down the knife and leaned against the fridge. He unwrapped the steak from its Seran wrap and ran his tongue across it, sucking it like a popsicle. Across from him, Eleanor found her way to a chair and sat, still trying in vain to stem the bleeding. Her lips were moving, silent pleas for her daughter to save her, to come to her senses and call 911, declarations of love and forgiveness. "Sorry, mom," the demon said. "I'm not a lipreader."

"What is going on, it's the middle of the –"

Mark stomped down the spiral stairs and into the kitchen, still rubbing sleep out of his eyes. He didn't have a chance to see his wounded wife before slipping on the pool of blood. Both of his legs caught air, feet higher than his head, and then the back of his skull cracked against the tile. Eleanor was so much in the throes of her own death that she didn't notice her husband's fall as life twitched out of her.

Nyhiloteph fell to his knees over Mark's unconscious body, as if he was about to perform CPR. Instead, the demon opened his mouth and bit into his neck with Adrienne's perfect teeth. The suckling and smacking went on for nearly an hour.

The half-frozen steak sat on the counter, nestled in a ball of shrink wrap. It could wait until tomorrow.

Chapter 19

Nyhiloteph waited four hours to call for help.

"Jack," he sobbed, "something happened and everything's all fucked up."

Jackson's muffled voice from the receiver: "Calm down, what happened?"

"I...I came ho...I mean, I was just about to leave for school and my...Adrienne's mother c-confronted me, she was onto us, I mean, like, she suspected something and I don't know what happened, I lost control of myself, I..."

Jackson heard a convincing series of hysterical, heaving breaths, though from my end it was clear the demon was cackling.

"Lucy!"

"I was just trying to get away but she grabbed me, and I don't know what happened, I think she's dead..."

"What!?" Jackson yelled.

Nyhiloteph hiccupped a sob. "And then her dad came down and -"

"You killed Adrienne's dad?"

Nyhiloteph sniffed. "And her mom. But Jack, it wasn't my fault - he slipped on the blood!"

"Blood?!" Jackson shrieked. "Lucy, what did you do?"

"I don't remember!"

You remembered pretty good twenty seconds ago, I thought.

"Please, just come."

And Jackson re-assured him that he would; he was only a few minutes away and heading right over.

Nyhiloteph blew his nose. "Can you bring the guys? I...I don't think we can do this alone."

"Do what?"

"We need to clean this up, Jackson. We have to get rid of them."

Dead air. I hoped this would finally be a bridge too far. But Jackson recovered himself and just said, "Okay."

Nyhiloteph sent emails from Mark and Eleanor's accounts, telling their assistants that they were heading on a wilderness retreat to save their marriage following revelations of infidelity, and would be unreachable for the foreseeable future. Then he washed his face and brushed the blood from his teeth. He re-applied Adrienne's makeup but wiped it off. It wouldn't do to look too put together. Throwing the stained towel to the ground, he pressed Adrienne's face to the mirror. It looked clammy and haggard, smeared lip gloss and eyeshadow completing the look. He bared his teeth, which showed no evidence of cannibalism. He looked, for all intents and purposes, like a teenage girl who'd suffered an ordeal. He cupped a hand to smell his breath and crinkled his nose; too fresh. A crack in the illusion. He'd go downstairs and take a bite of the counter steak to foul it up again.

Nyhiloteph nearly made Mark's mistake, saving himself from a spill by catching the countertop. The tableau was mostly how he'd left it, Adrienne's mother sitting up with clasped hands sliding down her throat, her father gored on the floor. Nyhiloteph chewed while he pondered. Eleanor's condition was consistent with what he'd told Jackson, but Mark's demise was no mere head wound. Back up the stairs. He stripped the master bed, bringing sheets down by the armful. This time he did slip on Eleanor's blood, pitching forward and sending the bundle flying across the room. He landed on his chin and elbows, the wind whooshing out of him. Swearing under his breath, he stood up and shook his arms out, tongue massaging aching teeth. He hadn't felt physical pain in ages, and it hurt.

Pillow waddled in as Nyhiloteph was wrapping up Mark, "for decency." The demon watched as the little dog started to lap up the blood on the floor. "I guess killing you right now would strain my credibility," he said, and Pillow woofed in agreement.

Adrienne lived in a slightly upscale section of the neighbourhood, where the houses were big and new, backyards augmented with inground pools and tennis nets and covered patios. Her parents could have afforded somewhere much more opulent, but they'd wanted her to grow up normal. So much for that.

The backyard gate was open when the boys pulled in. "Should we be parking here?" Abdul asked.

Jackson repeated his mantra: "We're just friends paying a visit."

"Then why do we have to sneak in through the backyard?" Abdul said.

"I don't know, man, she's not thinking straight."

"No shit," Brady chimed in, chuckling absently.

"Are you high?" Abdul demanded.

Brady shrugged. "Wouldn't you be, in my situation?"

"We are in your situation, and neither of us are high!" He threw up his hands and clapped them back down. "This is just great, not only are we...do you have drugs on you right now?"

"Why do you ask?"

"Argghh! Don't you think we're in enough shit already, without bringing illicit substances along?"

"Guys, stop screaming," Jackson pleaded.

"I think if we get caught doing whatever we're doing, no one's gonna care about an eighth of weed."

Abdul clenched his fists. "If we get pulled over and you smell like pot, the cops have reasonable grounds to search the car. You've screwed us."

"Dude, it's frigging legal."

"Not for minors!"

"You're the only minor here."

"Legal age is 19, dumbass."

"No one gets arrested for..."

"Guys!" Jackson snapped, shutting them both up. "No one is going to get pulled over. No one is going to get searched, because no one has any reason to suspect that anything bad has happened. We're a group of friends picking another friend up for school."

"And parking in her driveway well after the bell rings."

"What, you think the truancy officer's gonna come get you?"

"Shut up, Brady! Why did we even bring him?"

Jackson rested his fingertips atop the bridge of his nose, feeling a headache pulse. "Lucy asked."

"Lucy asked?"

"Yes, that's why were here, isn't it?"

Abdul narrowed his eyes. "She asked specifically for both of us?"

"Yes. Now let's get a move on, maybe we can get this done before the second bell."

Brady coughed. "I love your can-do attitude, man."

Adrienne's back lawn was immaculate, grass lush but short, a tiled gazebo taking up the corner and a clear blue pool sprawling across the rest of the yard. A top-of-the-line BBQ sat at the foot of the spacious wooden patio that led to a glass sliding door, dotted with red.

"Holy shit," Brady said. "This is real."

Abdul grabbed Brady's shoulder to steady him, and to give himself another reason not to run away again. Jackson went ahead, wincing as he grabbed the door handle. He hadn't thought to bring gloves. It slid open smoothly. He made a choking sound.

Adrienne's mother was still in her chair, a thick streak of blood painted from her throat to her lap. A burrito of blankets was rolled up on the floor, secured with duct tape. In the centre of the scene was their friend, looking sheepish, hands stained reddish brown.

Brady puked on the floor, and everyone simultaneously thought, *Great, more DNA.*

Abdul stood frozen at the window until he'd scanned the whole scene twice and asked, not, "What did you do?" but, "How long ago did this happen?"

"Does it matter?" asked Nyhiloteph pathetically.

"Come on, guys," Jackson said, supressing his gag reflex, "let's clean this up and get out of here."

"I'm not touching that," Brady said, trembling.

"Come on, man."

"He's got a point," Abdul said, gesturing towards the puddle of vomit. "We can't risk any more of that. Brady, you're going to wipe up all this blood while Jackson and I deal with the..." He trailed off. "Adrienne, where do you keep your cleaning supplies? Sorry, Lucy – where did the de Keyser family keep the cleaning supplies?"

Nyhiloteph sat on the back of the couch, doing his best impression of a devastated daze. "Under the sink."

Brady shuffled past the carnage to the kitchen sink, taking his time rifling through containers of ant killer and suede protector, as if hoping Jackson and Abdul would be done by the time he found the right chemical.

Since Adrienne's father came pre-packaged, they started with him. Abdul grabbed him by the feet, leaving Jackson the head, which he conked on the edge of the kitchen island as they carried him like a mattress out of the room. "Watch it, I'm walking backwards here."

A red stain was seeping through the sheets, near where Mark's throat would have been.

"Umm…how exactly did he die?" Abdul asked.

Nyhiloteph, still playing possum, didn't answer. Jackson replied instead, echoing the demon: "Does it matter?"

"I thought you said he hit his head."

"That's what Lucy told me." Jackson was whispering now.

"Would a head wound bleed this much?"

"Oh yeah, the head bleeds like crazy."

Abdul frowned. He wasn't a spatter expert, but the blood stain looked too low to have started at the back of Mark's skull.

"Watch the hurl."

Leaving the house made them both nervous, and Jackson nearly overstepped and fell into the pool. It was even worse once they left the backyard. I held my breath the entire distance from the gate to the car, silently echoing Abdul's moan of, "Why the heck didn't we back in?"

Jackson let the body drop, its head hitting the concrete with a thud that made me wince even though I knew the man within the sheets was dead. Jackson patted his hips, face falling. "Oh no."

"What?"

"My keys."

"Where are they?"

Jackson shoved his hands in both his pockets, digging as deep as they could go, and plumbed his back pockets for good measure. "Did I have them when I went in the house?" he asked.

"How am I supposed to know?"

"Maybe I left them on the counter..."

"Please don't tell me we have to go back in there."

Jackson peered into the driver's side window, sighed, and said, "Found them."

They were in the ignition, locked in the car.

They stashed the body in the de Keysers' shed and waited forty-five minutes for the Canadian Automobile Association. Abdul didn't say a word the whole time. "You boys sure are late to class," the CAA rep observed, unlocking the car doors after scrutinizing Jackson's ID.

"Yep," Abdul said tersely.

"Oh well," the man smiled. "It's almost summer."

Jackson turned to retrieve the body as soon as the CAA car turned the corner; Abdul stopped him with a hand on his arm and made him wait another ten-count, just to be safe. Carefully propped shovels and rakes clattered to the ground as they pulled the wrapped body from the shed.

"We should have just buried them here," Abdul sighed.

"Don't be stupid."

Abdul bit back a retort.

"Pull the car out and back it in closer. We've been in plain sight too long already."

"Got it," Jackson snapped.

I stayed in the backyard to watch Abdul as Jackson maneuvered the car. He was staring at the fence, at nothing really, withdrawn into his own head. Into a rage that coursed through his veins or nervous system or whatever part of the anatomy carried emotion through the body, stiffening his back and clenching his fists. In years of knowing him, I'd never seen him angry until recently; now he rarely seemed to feel anything else.

Perhaps what had kept Abdul stoic despite years of being bullied and condescended to was his unwavering faith that he would be rewarded. Abdul was a straight A student and he'd bought into the nerd prophecy that he'd be employing his bullies one day, or at least buying fast food off them. As a consequence, he understood darn well, better than burned-out Brady or delusional Jackson, what they were at risk of losing if they were caught today. Sentencing instead of graduation, prison instead of university, parents no longer proud, decades of miserable confinement with only halfway houses and minimum wage to look forward to. Even if they somehow got away with this crime and he was presented the glittering future he'd worked for, would he still deserve it? Or would he be forever followed by the ghost of his childhood self, tapping him on the shoulder to remind him that he was an accomplice to murder? And that he'd been, in a way, partly responsible for it?

Abdul's thoughts were so loud he might as well have been screaming. I felt him cycle from anxiety to resentment to guilt, saw him running through lost pasts and forfeited futures: torturing himself with versions of the séance night where he'd stuck around to stop them from going through with it.

Weirdly enough, wading into Abdul's remorse was the closest I came to experiencing it myself. I don't know what that says about me.

"We're just moving some furniture," Jackson muttered as they carried the body to the car. I don't know if he was trying to comfort Abdul or himself.

"A long, thin piece of furniture wrapped in a sheet."

"A lamp," Jackson said.

"A lamp leaking blood."

"That's why they're getting rid of it. Now, heave."

They threw the body through the open hatch. It landed among Jackson's parents' camping supplies, just another securely-packaged mysterious object. Jackson sighed. "Okay. One down, one to go."

Abdul didn't move.

"You coming?"

"Jack, why are we doing this?"

Jackson scanned the street, paranoid. He gestured to the front seat of the car and they climbed in. Jackson didn't reply until both doors were shut. "Because she's our friend and she's in trouble."

"So, is this going to be like a weekly thing now? Every time someone pisses her off, are we going to have a body to dispose of?"

"She's just going through a lot," Jackson replied, staring at the garage door instead of meeting Abdul's eyes.

"The Lucy we knew would never have killed anyone. Did she come back with a taste for it or something?"

"You don't have to be here," Jackson snapped. "Leave if you want, we can handle this."

"Can you?" Abdul asked. "Because Brady can't even look at that scene without throwing up. Which is the normal reaction to something like this. I don't know…"

"What?"

Abdul inhaled. "I know you're really far in, but I don't know how you can bring yourself to participate in this."

"You're right here next to me," Jackson reminded him.

"And I don't understand that either. I don't know how we reached this point."

Jackson finally met his eyes. "Believe me, I know this is crazy. And I know Lucy's different - she came back from the dead, and I guess that screws you up. But she's still Lucy and she needs us. And you know she'd do exactly the same for us if the situations were reversed."

It was Abdul's turn to avert his gaze. "I guess she's not really morally culpable, if this was just a temporary insanity. She doesn't deserve to be locked up. And if Adrienne ever gets her body back, she doesn't either."

Jackson nodded, buying into it. "Besides, we were the ones who got her into this situation."

"No," Abdul replied, stepping out of the car. "You were."

They came back in to find Brady sitting on the floor, surrounded by dozens of multicoloured spray bottles.

"You haven't started yet?" Abdul wheezed.

Brady's face scrunched indignantly. "I've never scrubbed a floor before! I don't know what to use!"

Abdul turned on Nyhiloteph, sprawled on the sofa and staring at the ceiling. "You couldn't have helped? You got us into this and you're just gonna lie there?"

"Leave her alone!" Jackson said. "Can't you see she's in shock?"

Playing it up, Nyhiloteph muttered to himself. "I don't know what happened. We were talking one minute and…"

"Come on, let's get this over with. Same plan. Abdul, you and I will load up Adrienne's mom, drop them both at the dump. Brady, you clean, and we'll pick you up when we're done."

"Exactly," Brady chimed in unhelpfully. "We'll all do our thing, when this is all over we'll laugh about it."

"Sure," Abdul seethed.

"Adri-" Jackson blanched. "I mean, Lucy, do you have a second set of sheets?"

"Blanket on ottoman."

As Jackson passed the couch, Nyhiloteph shot up, like a movie vampire from its coffin. Jackson tensed up as the demon squeezed him tight. "Thank you," he breathed. "I know I've been a mess lately but I do appreciate you, I really do…"

Abdul looked at Brady, raising an eyebrow. Their expressions turned from befuddlement to disgust when Nyhiloteph stood on Adrienne's tip-toes, placed her hands on Jackson's cheeks, and leaned in for a kiss. The timing worked so everyone saw Nyhiloteph slip him some tongue.

Chapter 20

Artemis wasn't as disturbed as he should have been when I told him Nyhiloteph had killed Adrienne's parents and enlisted my friends in covering it up. "That's par for the course," he replied. "Magpies often destroy their host from the outside-in."

Since identifying Nyhiloteph in the demon encyclopedia, Artemis had devoted himself to finding out everything he could about his particular species. Nyhiloteph was one variation of something Artemis called a "magpie," which was a nicer way of saying "parasite."

"What do you mean by that?" I said, reclined on the wall shelf next to the partridge.

"Demons like Nyhiloteph tend to do everything possible to alter the conditions of their host's existence. Alienate their friends, slaughter their family, burn their village to the ground - basically, give them nothing to live for, making it less likely they'll fight to get their body back. After the conditions are right, the demon will consume the body itself. The host will become ill, you'll start to see self-mutilations, sometimes auto-cannibalism..."

I pulled the partridge closer. "What happens when the body dies, though? Does he have to find a new one?"

Artemis hummed. "The literature is unclear on that."

"Artemis."

"Some of the books say yes, which would actually be the ideal option."

"Fuck," I said. "What's the less-than-ideal option?"

He replied with a sort of vibrating exhale, which indicated I wouldn't like the answer.

"Why does Nyhiloteph even need a human body? He was able to kill you in spirit form. And he was obviously way stronger on his own – Adrienne could never have overpowered you like that. Why does he want her?"

"He draws power from her flesh. He's not meant to be on this plane; he's probably only able to manifest outside her body for a short period of time." Artemis shut the book, inserting a business card from the desk to mark his place. "That's why I'm hoping her eventual death will send him back to this limbo. Because there's a good chance that it won't."

"You're going to have to spell this out for me."

He cringed. "Like I said, the literature varies. But the impression I'm getting is that after Nyhiloteph's done feeding off Adrienne, his spirit will be able to survive on this plane permanently."

"Fuck, are you serious?"

"Probably not forever," Artemis clarified. "But he might be able to last for a decade, maybe a century."

"A century of Nyhiloteph doing his thing at full strength, with no inhibitions."

"Yep."

I gulped, trying to comprehend it but not wanting to. "So, we have no choice at all. We have to get him out before he kills her."

"Keep in mind," Artemis said, "if we force him out of that body, he'll have a few minutes of fight left in him in his super-strong, superhuman spirit form. I wouldn't want to be a living person in the vicinity when that happens."

"You're just full of good news today."

"Look on the bright side, that's the worst of it."

"Knock on wood," I said, just as someone knocked on the door.

I jumped, nudging the partridge off its perch; Artemis caught it before it could smash on the floor.

"Who the fuck could that be?"

"I don't know." Ducking his shoulders as if anyone outside would be able to see him, Artemis crept to the front door. He pressed his face to the frosted glass and recoiled. "Shit!"

"Who is it?"

"It's my fucking mother."

I thought you had no family, I was about to say, and then the visitor rapped on the glass. Had she seen him? I recalled my fruitless attempts to reach my own parents, and told myself there was no way she could.

"Arthur! I see you in there!"

Artemis winced.

"Your name is Arthur?" I asked.

"Shut up." His hiss was so shrill his mother could probably hear it through the wood.

"Arthur, I can hear you, too. We need to talk." Another round of tapping.

Artemis turned to me, his face an exaggerated mask of panic.

"Go out and talk to her," I said.

"No fucking way!"

"What if she thinks you're in distress and calls the cops? Just keep your distance and don't let her touch you."

He twisted in indecision, contorting his body in the dozen directions he could flee, before putting his hand on the knob. He opened the door a crack, just wide enough for his frame to fit through, and slammed it shut as soon as he was on the stoop, facing his mother.

She reached out to touch his arm. He stepped back sharply, pressed so close to the wall I feared he was going to slip through. She looked wounded.

Artemis didn't soften, but also couldn't meet her eyes. "What are you doing here?"

"I wanted to see you," she said.

He didn't reply.

"How are you?"

"Fine."

She eyed the door, expecting to be invited in. Artemis leaned against it protectively.

"Is there somewhere we can sit down?" she asked.

"I'm renovating."

She exhaled, an exasperated tic. She probably wasn't even aware she'd done it.

Artemis stiffened. "What, am I not supposed to make improvements on my business lest you decide to drop in?"

"No one's saying that, Arthur. We're not all lining up to persecute you."

"Oh?"

Her face crumpled. "Don't be like this. Is there somewhere we can talk?"

"No, there isn't. We can talk here." Artemis had not tried to leave the store since his death; I wasn't even sure he could.

"Your father's not well."

She meant to let the sentence hang, to give Artemis a chance to process it. To wait for his face to fall and his guard to drop. His retort was too quick for all that. "Wasn't that always apparent?"

"This is serious, Arthur."

He just hummed, in that way he does when he doesn't want to talk. I could hear the words he really wanted to say, feel the Herculean effort of holding them back. His back teeth clenched, biting down on the inside of his lip. "It's too late for this."

"Arthur." She looked down at the stoop. "We always tried to do what was best for you."

"What, making me homeless?"

"You're not being fair, son. We didn't..."

"Didn't what?" he snapped as she trailed off. "Don't try to say you didn't understand. I'm well aware you don't know shit about me."

"It was hard for us, too!" she yelled, fists clenching. She bit her lip, realizing she was losing the plot. When she spoke again her volume was down, but her voice was still a vibrato of emotion. "I just...he always loved you, and I would hate...hate for something to happen before you could settle things."

"Ha."

"Excuse me?"

Artemis took a deep breath, barking on the exhale. "You're worried that my father will die before we can reconcile, and I'll regret it for the rest of my life." He wasn't laughing anymore, chest heaving with throttled sobs. "Your timing isn't good at all."

I saw the image, formed in his mind, of Artemis flinging open the door to reveal his battered and rotting corpse, then floating off gleefully as his mother screamed in anguish.

"Don't even think about it," I growled.

His mother perked up like she'd heard me. "Is there a man in there?"

"None of your business." Artemis shook his head, got a hold of himself. "Listen, this isn't going to work. You could have come by any time in the past fourteen years. You can't just show up now that you want something and make demands of me."

"You had our number," she replied acidly.

"You were the parent," he pointed out, his past tense pointed.

"We weren't perfect, okay? Is that what you want me to admit? But I'm here now, offering an olive branch. Does that count for nothing?"

Artemis's voice quivered. "It's too fucking late."

Not risking another second, he opened the door and started to slip through. "What do you want me to tell your father when I go see him in the hospital today?" his mother demanded, just before he closed it.

"You can tell him I'm dead to him."

Click.

Artemis's corpse rippled with maggots. It had collapsed under its own weight over the past few days; its knees no longer supported a kneeling position, and its chest now touched the ground. The mashed face had lost what little shape had remained after the beating; it may as well have been glued to the floorboard.

Artemis stood with eyes squeezed shut, face buried in a bookshelf, as if trying to disappear into the broken body behind him. When that didn't work, he grunted and peeled himself away, his face detaching from the spines with a slick ripping sound. I gagged. He was wearing his wounds again, and they were even leaving a residue.

"Do you want Meat Loaf?" I asked.

He touched his cheek, and his fingers stuck to it. "Shit." He yanked the fingers away, examining the congealed substance clinging to them, and turned to inspect the books, groaning when he saw the black smears. "Yes, please put the record on."

Artemis's face swelled with the music, and he was more or less repaired by the second chorus of "More Than You Deserve." I pretended not to notice he was singing along.

"Would you have gone to see him if you could?" I asked as the song changed.

"Meat Loaf?"

"No, your father. In the hospital."

A moment of hesitation, then: "No way. Not after what they did to me."

I heard the true answer in his head, and it made me indescribably sad.

Even after everything, absolutely, yes.

Chapter 21

Mr. Jones sat with a stack of photocopied printouts to his left, a box of paper clips to his right. Licking his finger, he counted out three pages and clipped them together, adding them to another pile that wobbled like the Tower of Pisa. He was not technically authorized to make so many copies of this set of sheet music, but what ASCAP didn't know wouldn't hurt them.

Jones liked these quiet moments of work before the halls were filled with chatter. As a music teacher, he had more noise tolerance than most, but could only get administrative work done when the school was empty, his only company a framed photograph of the orange-furred Maine Coon who awaited him at home.

But today, an odour plagued him, a fetid note of decay that had him convinced he'd tracked in roadkill from the parking lot. But he hadn't, and he felt gaslit by his pristine soles and the neat, empty room that no one had entered since the custodian mopped up the night before. A room where food was banned, even during lunchtime practices, guaranteeing no errant slice of ham or glob of mayonnaise or rolled away grape would sully his rehearsal space.

Until today.

From the wall-mounted landline, Jones dialled the custodian. He got an answering machine. It was still an hour before morning band practice, too early for anyone else to be in. He'd forgotten. But as he leaned against the door, the origin of the scent became clearer: the closet where all the instruments were stored. Perhaps a student had surreptitiously scarfed their lunch there, and something had been left to rot. Jones frowned. That closet, more than anywhere else, was supposed to be spotless, clean and climate controlled. Any slip in professionalism in the band's environment would be replicated in their performance.

The smell hit him like a wave as soon as he opened the door, but it was the sight that broke the music teacher's heart.

Clarinets and flutes lay in a disorganized heap on the floor, dinged and dented, never to sing so sweetly again. The snare drums at the back had their skins slashed. All three bass guitars had been unstrung, their oak necks snapped. Who would do such a thing? Who could even be capable? And the stench - it seemed to be radiating off the brass section. Plugging his nose, he stood in front of the instruments, gleaming gold hidden under black lids, like cold and beautiful women in caskets. Did some foulness now lurk there, too, waiting to be released?

But one of the cases was already open a crack. The largest one. Jones removed the lid.

The stench filled the room like steam. Its source was greenish-pink and lacking any discernible shape. My first guess was a dead animal, perhaps one of the squirrels that regularly made their last stand at the intersection where the parking lot met the street. Other, more depraved options crossed my mind: the music teacher's beloved cat, or Adrienne's loyal little Pillow, who I'd seen Nyhiloteph cruelly kick down the stairs.

Releasing his pinched nostrils – fingers were insufficient, now – Jones leaned over the case and reeled back, face purpling with rage. "Disgusting."

Someone had dumped a pound of raw ground beef into the bell of the tuba.

Chapter 22

Before Nyhiloteph made his entrance, Room 104 was so quiet you could hear the clock tick. The Tom Thomson Chess Club was up against visitors from A.Y. Jackson Secondary to see who'd progress to the city finals. With the defeat of club president George Abed, our hopes were pinned on his VP Shannah Gibson, the tremor of her hand like the straining muscles of Atlas.

The faculty supervisor sat with his feet up among the re-arranged desks at the back of the room. A spread of snacks and papers for grading formed a barrier between him and his charges; he was a student teacher, only a few years older than the seniors, and the set-up gave the unfortunate impression of a child's fort.

There was a surplus of empty chairs, but Nyhiloteph took the seat right next to him. The demon's makeup had improved dramatically since his first day of school smear job. Thick black wings with neon green shadow, accentuated by a dark brown lipstick that reminded me of dried blood – still too bold a look for Adrienne, but at least the brushwork was even, the lines precise. "Hi, Scott. I see you got stuck marking the in-class essays."

"It's Mr. Anderson," the student teacher corrected, making himself seem three years younger.

"Sure."

A spectator shushed them. When Scott wasn't looking, Nyhiloteph swiped a sip from his half-drank fountain pop.

I kept expecting him to knock over the game board at some crucial point. But the demon observed respectfully, even joining the applause as Shanna took her opponent's king. I'd known Shanna to be high-achieving and ambitious, though this was the first time I'd seen her looking genuinely pleased with anything. Here she was in her glory, feted by her teammates, including the boy who'd beat her for the presidency by a single vote, hands for shaking thrust in her direction.

The crackling of the PA interrupted the revelry. "Please listen up for this very special announcement. We just received word that the Tom Thomson drama department's spellbinding production of *Sweeney Todd* has been nominated for four Cappie Awards. The nominees are…"

Shanna rolled her eyes as the names were listed. "We interrupt this programming to kiss the ass of Tom Thompson's cabal of drama queens and over-actors…" The chess club chortled, improvising their own additions.

Nyhiloteph took in the discontent, only speaking up after the last of the chess kids got their cracks in. "Aren't you happy for their success?"

Shanna snorted, noticing the cool girl interloper for the first time. "Ecstatic. Now, what are the odds they do a special news bulletin for our win?"

George held up a partially clenched fist, his thumb and forefinger forming a zero. "Never have before."

"That can't be true," Nyhiloteph protested. Goading them.

"You don't think?" Shanna snorted. "I mean, look around. Sports trophies everywhere, the art students have their paintings up in the foyer, and the drama club has not one, but two display cases dedicated to them and all the awards they win. Which, good for them, whatever, but we get relegated to a dingy classroom, no support, and no credit. Last year they didn't even put us in the yearbook."

"That was because George gave us the wrong date for the photo day," another member pointed out.

Shanna flushed. "Yeah, well, if the drama club hadn't showed up for their photo, you can bet they would have given them another date."

"The drama kids are the elite tier of geek," George added, only half-joking.

"Not even," Shanna said. "They're the pretty popular kids, except they actually have some talent."

"No offense, Adrienne," George added.

Nyhiloteph blew a strand of hair out of his face, pretending to be deep in thought. "You know, I'm planning Grad Oscars this year. There's a category for student athletes – what if we nominated some people from the academic teams, too? You guys, Reach for the Top, the Science Olympians..."

"Why are you so obsessed with Grad Oscars?" I muttered. Was it just an Adrienne tic he'd seized on for his impression - the way she used to think a made-up award would make everything okay?

"That would certainly make a point," Shanna replied, thinking about it. "You'd do that?"

"Absolutely. It's about time someone stood up for you." Quieter, leaning close to Shanna's ear, he added: "But you also need to stand up for yourself, don't you think?"

On the way to class, Shanna crossed paths with Alana Dickinson, Mrs. Lovett from *Sweeney*. At the instant of intersection, Shanna stuck out her foot. Alana tripped and pitched forward.

I should say, she started by pitching forward. Partway through the fall she veered sharply to the right, smashing face-first into a display case. The glass cracked against her temple and her chin bounced off the edge.

Shanna froze, waiting for the the flying of fingers, the cries of, *You did that on purpose!* But as always, Alana got all the attention. Her face, when she pulled herself up, was a bloody fright mask, shards of glass sticking out of her cheeks. Her nose was bent to the right. When she gained the presence of mind to smile reassuringly, her front teeth were cracked.

The spiderwebs in the glass grew to consume the whole pane, obscuring everything behind it. Props and programs, photos from *Sweeney*, and painted gold statuettes from drama seasons past, honouring the excellence of the cast and crew.

Every time Nyhiloteph made a friend, something bad happened.

On Tuesday, he commiserated with honour roll perennial Paul Sharma, who'd gotten his first ever B after being forcibly partnered with Carter Daniels. "I gave him one job – read what I wrote and write the conclusion – and he couldn't even do that right." Later that day, Paul knocked over a beaker in science class, giving Carter a chemical burn.

On Wednesday, Nyhiloteph sat with Destiny, the friendless goth girl who spent every lunch period reading by her locker. Destiny stuck out her foot as a cheerleader walked by, not looking up from *Good Omens* as the girl sprawled across the tile.

On Thursday, Nyhiloteph was helping proofread the yearbook before the editor submitted her final draft. The version sent to the printers that day included a full-colour photo from my fiery crash under the heading "A Night to Remember."

Chapter 23

"Nyhiloteph's befriending all the high school outsiders."

"Oh gosh," Artemis exclaimed, hunched over a notepad. "I'd hate to see him fall into a bad crowd. Ponyboy and Johnny are okay, but that Dally's bad news."

I kept talking. Sarcasm meant Artemis was listening. "He's been hanging around the geeks and the alt kids – the ones he assumes must have an axe to grind. He gains their confidence, gets them talking about grudges and slights, and then he...I don't know, he gets in their heads, makes them do things they wouldn't normally do. Helps them get revenge."

"A friend to the outcast and a liberator of the oppressed." His pencil whispered ceaselessly.

"Most of them aren't even that angry. Not until he talks to them." I collapsed into the nearest armchair, propping my heels up on a stack of pagan periodicals. "And he's been weirdly nice to the student teacher, too. Flirty, almost. Like, what'll that get him? It's not like Scott controls the final marks."

"Please don't put your feet there."

"I'm insubstantial, they're not actually touching anything."

"I know, just, have some decency. Or buy your own store to haunt."

I got up, but rebelled by flipping through his precious record collection.

"*Bat Out of Hell Three*? I didn't even know they made a second one."

"Philistine."

The cover for this one had the muscled blonde hero swooping through an inferno, broadsword in hand, to rescue a delicate damsel from a gigantic fire-breathing bat that took up half the sleeve.

"I thought Nyhiloteph was trying not to make friends," Artemis said, startling me.

"I think he was just pushing away Adrienne's friends."

Artemis hmmed. The bat's fire singed the hero's hair before it was beheaded.

I'd read a story once where the monster was vanquished, and the damsel wept.

"What?" I asked.

The medium drummed on his desk. "Didn't you say Nyhiloteph was kind of clueless? Hitting on guys who know you're gay, that sort of thing? How is he suddenly so adept at navigating high school social dynamics? That's not the sort of thing you pick up in a couple days."

A chill seized my spine. "Or a lifetime, in my case," I replied, the dumb quip a placeholder for my whirl of thoughts as I slipped out of the Grimoire the way I'd come.

Pop-punk, of all things, blared from the mini speaker on the end table. Adrienne was sprawled on her unmade bed, fingers massaging a trembling Pillow. The dog's teeth chattered; when it let a whine escape, Adrienne pinched it, her wet nail polish staining its locks.

I say Adrienne, in this case, because Nyhiloteph was outside of her.

Their bodies were entwined, the demon's a contorted, not-quite-solid form. At his edges, spindly fur hardened into something shiny and metallic, which linked to Adrienne's joints like the gears of some great machine. Beneath Nyhiloteph's oil-stink, Adrienne smelled like spiced daisies in a bed of charcoal. A perfume with notes of bliss and evil.

The contents of her closet were piled on the floor, still clinging to their hangers. Floating above the heap, Nyhiloteph was using his claws to distress pairs of black hose. He tossed the ruined garments to Adrienne, who wriggled into them to inspect the stylized tears, sometimes using her own nails – gleaming newly onyx- to rip them wider. "It's such slim pickings here," she lamented. "I can't believe how square I used to dress."

Adrienne was alive? And getting a rock-chick makeover?

Her blonde hair, usually straightened or gently waving, was a nest of wild curls. Her lipstick was dark purple and her nostril was bleeding where a pin had been shoved through, an inelegant home piercing. Overturned in her lap was a jewellery box decorated with blackbirds and cherry blossoms, the silver clasp broken off. Jewellery she'd sorted was scattered across the bed, diamonds and costume pieces alike getting lost in the folds of sheets. Occasionally she'd untangle a particular necklace and scowl, before throwing it against the wall hard enough to dent the plaster.

A strand of while gold soared through me, along with a flow of alien memories. A family heirloom, gifted by Mark to Eleanor on their 20th anniversary. Eleanor's nose crinkling as she clicked the box shut, saying, "Nothing like a hand-me-down to show how much you love someone." An argument, treading a well-worn path of hurt. The anniversary party, Adrienne flitting from guest-to-guest with a forced smile, assuring relatives and colleagues that Mark would join them soon, in between surreptitious visits to the master bedroom to beg her sulking father to make an appearance. The memory was a subcutaneous needle that slipped painlessly into my flesh but expanded into a burning ache once it crossed the barrier, Adrienne's anguish entering me and becoming mine. I let out a moan.

Nyhiloteph heard and looked my way.

My flight back to the store was so violent I almost flattened myself against the front door. I felt the wood conk me on the head as I merged through, tumbling heels-over-head to crumple on the floor, shaking more violently than Adrienne's lapdog. *He didn't see me*, I told myself. *He hasn't noticed me yet, why would he notice me now*, though I knew this time had been decidedly different. Lying to myself to still my nerves.

Artemis's music choice didn't help: a frantic, jittery metal anthem, Meat's rock-n-roll howl delivering a paranoid diatribe backed by screeching violins, galloping power chords and tolling bells. My own fault – he'd put on *Bat Out of Hell III*.

Artemis looked at me expectantly, and I held up my wait finger. As the operatic din shook the store, a new album cover entered my head, nothing Richard Corben or Julie Bell ever drew. A pile-up of all the rejects at Tom Thompson High School – the punks and metalheads, the club-joining kids, the brainiacs, the ones who considered trivia and board games to be sports, the goths and the loners – all wretched, emaciated, clothes slashed and torn, reaching up for their saviour. Looming over the squirming masses, just out of reach, a woman with a pin-up body, expression imperious and eyes black as coal. A demon with a woman's form, rallying his troops.

"Adrienne was the nicest person in the world," I moaned, head in my hands.

She'd never been more than a friend-of-a-friend to me, but her altruism was evident even in fleeting interactions. The whole class was always invited to her elementary school birthday parties. She complimented people on their presentations, even if they'd bombed. If she found someone crying in the bathroom, she'd have a go-pack of Kleenex handy so they didn't have to weep into toilet paper. She hung around with some mean girls, but I'd never met anyone who didn't like her. By senior year, Adrienne was the undisputed Patron Saint of Tom Thompon High. She organized dances, spirit days, and charity fundraisers. She dragged friends to every game, concert, or play and cheered even when someone botched a line or missed a free throw. When she co-edited the yearbook, she made sure the candid pages weren't totally dominated by the cool kid cliques. If you partnered with her on a project, she somehow managed to defer to the group while taking on the lion's share of the work. Granted, she could never bring herself to cast a tie-breaking vote and she'd turtle in a conflict, but lack of assertiveness isn't a sin. Until it's a demon who's pushing you around.

Now she was Nyhiloteph's double agent. Every confidence she'd ever kept, the insights her empathy had earned her, everything she knew about our classmates' dreams, fears, and resentments, was now intel. The accelerant the demon needed to set the school ablaze.

Alienate their friends, slaughter their family, burn their village to the ground. Nyhiloteph had done some of that already; with Adrienne consulting on psychological warfare, the village would set itself on fire.

Chapter 24

Principal Marsters had a thick salt-and-pepper moustache and always wore a full tracksuit to school. He'd dreamed of being a gym teacher but had been honoured with unwanted promotions. Nalo and Kerri settled in the two plastic chairs facing the principal's desk. If they'd been nonchalant about this invitation on the way in, his demeanour unsettled that before he even said a word. Marsters usually lounged casually in his desk chair, leaning back with his hands behind his head and feet propped on one of the side-drawer handles. But today he was sitting up and leaning forward as he asked, "Do you want to tell me what you meant by the phrase, 'Adrienne's been a super-bitch since she hooked up with that car crash guy?'"

They couldn't compose themselves quickly enough. Shocked recognition. Widened eyes, quickened blinking, sudden tensing up of muscles. For a fraction of an instant, I felt Nalo's heart stop.

"We don't know what you're talking about," Kerri's chest had turned bright red, and beads of sweat were running down her neck.

The principal smirked. "Neither of you?"

His lips a tight line under his moustache, Marsters adjusted his computer monitor so it faced them. Blown up like a novelty cheque was a screenshot of a series of text messages. The identity of the recipient had been digitally blacked out, so the only names visible were Nalo and Kerri's.

I saw the girls' minds moving like hamster wheels, wondering what to say and who'd ratted them out. The name popped into their heads at the exact same time, the only girl in the group chat who wasn't sitting in the office with them: Michelle.

That bitch, Kerri thought.

Marsters looked down at them expectantly. Almost like he was enjoying this. I found myself wishing he'd been the one handling my bullies, back when I had human enemies.

Nalo finally spoke up. "That was a private conversation, actually."

"It certainly didn't stay private," Marsters replied.

"We were just…" Kerri said.

"Concerned about your friend?" Marsters replied.

Nalo ignored the mockery in his tone. "Well, she had been acting strange since the accident, and –"

Marsters stopped her with a raised hand. "You girls are very lucky," the principal said. "Because I think these messages are disgusting and cruel, and they aren't the only ones I've seen from you two."

Kerri had taken on so much colour, I feared the blood-heat would melt her chair.

"Your other statements in this chat are so vicious I don't even want to engage with them. I don't want to read them aloud lest I take on some of the taint."

Shit, what was in this group chat? And how long had it been going on for? I'd have assumed Adrienne would be part of any forum these girls would use – unless they made a new chat to exclude her, post-possession. Or maybe even post-accident.

"If I'd had the final word, I would have barred you two from every extracurricular, including the Grad Committee. Contacted the university admissions offices to let them know your past involvement shouldn't be taken as evidence of good character."

He paused, let them take that in. "But Adrienne, of all people, interceded for you. She said she needs your help with Grad Oscars, begged me not to kick you off the Committee." The right edge of his mouth twitched up. "She said that 'working with her to celebrate other students' would be the most appropriate penance for you."

I watched the girls' faces when he said that, expecting relief or maybe even shame. Instead, I was surprised. If they'd looked fearful before, when they only expected punishment, what I now saw in their eyes, in their stiffened postures and the tension in their jaws, was terror. Not horror-movie-final-girl-screaming-through-the-trees terror – nothing Marsters would notice - but the trapped desperation of lambs by a butcher's block.

Did they understand why, I wondered? Why Marsters' commandment to maintain the status quo – to keep spending time with their old friend Adrienne – now seemed like a mini death sentence?

Marsters stood, dismissing them. "I'm not sure I agree with that, but it'll certainly give you less time to spend tearing people down."

I have to wonder if some bullying has a deeper purpose. Not to punish, but to safeguard. Maybe some people have retained an instinctual warning system, the way deer can sense, without seeing, a wolf in the bushes. I never had that sixth sense – I've always been too much of a people-pleaser – but Nalo and Kerri clearly did. Adrienne gave them the creeps, and they reacted commensurate with their maturity levels, but also their circumstances. They couldn't kill, and in a government-mandated school setting they couldn't even flee, so they used the only weapons they had: ostracization, mockery, intimidating displays of group power.

Of course, when the predator acts on the urges he's always harboured, they'll say he snapped from all the bullying.

"Will you let up?" Artemis snapped, me not even halfway through the theory. "The popular bitches in your school are not possessed of some innate evolutionary creep-sensing radar. They're just bitches, and they're like that to the nice people as well as to the creeps and the assholes." He slammed his book back open to the page he'd been marking with his finger. "I don't know why you think this high school shit fucking matters. Newsflash, you've graduated."

I felt like he'd kicked me out of his brain again. And I'd thought I was saying something halfway interesting.

"Do you never miss it?" I asked, chastened.

"High school?" he replied, incredulous.

"Yeah."

"Fuck, no."

"I do sometimes," I admitted.

"That's because you see it as a missed opportunity."

I assumed he meant because I'd died young and lost everything I'd been building towards, but he added, "Because you were a dork who wanted school to be like it is in the movies."

"I was not," I argued, not convincingly, trying to forget the yearning feeling when I watched cheerleader chick flicks and *Buffy, The Vampire Slayer.*

"You're literally getting a peer award for dying," he reminded me. "That is your legacy here."

"I would've been up for a better award if I hadn't died," I retorted, although I had no evidence to back that up. "It's just, I'm now out of the running for anything with 'Most Likely To' in the title."

"That's my point. You were all potential. You never actually achieved anything."

"Oh, come on, she could probably quote all the *Star Wars* movies."

Artemis and I whirled around. Nyhiloteph was standing in front of the door – his demonic form, fully visible. I'd seen him this way before, in Jackson's bedroom and in the woods, but Artemis hadn't yet. Even with both feet on the floor, his head grazed the ceiling. He left a trail of slime when he moved.

"*Star Trek*," I corrected.

"Of course, of course. I bet you were the only girl in school who watched it. So unique." I felt my cheeks burn red. "You always wanted to be different, didn't you, Lucy? Is that why you and this waste-of-space get along?"

"Hey!" Artemis yelped.

"Did you gain weight?" I snapped.

"I'm bigger in every way that matters," Nyhiloteph replied, his flaccid penis unrolling to flop on the ground.

"Your new bestie kick you out?" I asked. "I'm afraid we can't offer you a place to crash."

Nyhiloteph chuckled, the reverberation rattling shelves, making glass tinkle. "My dear Adrienne's a willing host. I've been showing her a better time than she's ever had."

"Did you break the news you're planning to kill her?"

This time his laugh was a shrill, rolling cackle that put a hairline crack in the window, sent volumes toppling from shelves and shelves slipping out of their brackets. A book fell open on Artemis' desk, pages flapping with the artificial breeze. "Why would I ever do that? Adrienne and I are friends. But you've never had a real one of those, have you? Yours have all forgotten you."

I bristled. "My friends tried to save me."

"Your friends who you haunted and lured?" His voice sharpened into yet another of its iterations: a ragged banshee shriek that wouldn't have been out of place in a black metal song. "Don't you get it? I've alwaysss been here. Who do you think gave Adrienne her little fit behind the wheel? Why that precissse inssstant?"

That shut me up.

The demon continued, each s a long hiss: "I knew you, Lucy Sssteinberg. I knew you'd force your ssso-called friendssss to prove their loyalty, while deluding yoursssself that you were helping them. I knew they'd be weak enough to obey you, and that they wouldn't care enough about the resssult to do it correctly. That they'd merely go through the motionss and call me inssssstead."

"Bullshit," I said, recalling the extremes the boys had gone to for me. The degradations they'd willingly suffered in the woods. The memory tasted like curdled milk.

Nyhiloteph shrunk into a lumpy caricature of Adrienne, skin ruched and wrinkled, eyes black and watery, lips blue like a corpse just pulled from a river. "Did it really never occur to you that you bewitched them?"

Bewitched. A word I'd used to describe Jackson's altered state. Now this demon was saying I'd done that?

His Adrienne skin wriggled and shifted as the impression evened out, every blink draining the black from his eyes until they were a grey that could almost pass for Adrienne's blue. His plan doused me like a gallon of ice water. Nyhiloteph wasn't just hiding within Adrienne – he was learning to be her.

"Only one of us has a genuine bone," he bragged, and I couldn't discern if it was a double entendre or another botched idiom. "I could have snuffed Adrienne out like a candle. Instead, I liberated her. I destroyed everything that ever held her back. No tricks, just mutual benefit."

"You murdered her family," I whispered, my voice the swishing of bugs' legs. "And you're going to eat her alive her as soon as she's no longer useful to you."

"Do you have wax in your ears?" Nyhiloteph said, his blue pools surveying the room. "Or just reading too many old books?"

Artemis flushed and started to shrivel, maggots poking out of his cheeks.

"Might want to invest in a new edition, Artie. Yes, in the past I might have eaten and ran, but those were more faithful times. If you possessed someone too long, the witchfinders got suspicious. But I outlived them all. And there's so many other people to devour. I don't have to rush."

I hated how brilliant it was. With Adrienne's shell, he could keep the con going indefinitely.

The demon flipped his blonde hair, flashing white teenage teeth. "See you later, losers."

Artemis didn't say anything for a long time after the demon left. Then: "You watched Star Trek?"

"Big Trekkie," I replied, numb.

"See?" he concluded, the maggots slithering back into his face. "Dork."

"Hey, Lucy?"

I almost jumped. "Yeah?"

"I didn't mean...that thing I said. I was kidding."

"I know."

"I run my mouth sometimes."

"I also know that."

"Seriously," Artemis insisted. "I was being unfair. You were a teenager. I don't know what anyone could have expected you to have achieved at that age."

"Thanks," I said dryly, though I took his point. "I figured you were projecting a little there."

He snorted. "Thirty sneaks up on you."

"That's one thing I'll never have to worry about."

Artemis laughed at that. It was a long and giddy peal, not unlike the demon's in some ways, except it didn't rattle any shelves.

Chapter 25

Adrienne – Nyhiloteph? – I'll operate on the assumption that the demon was in the driver's seat – showed up to school the next Monday wearing a sheer camisole as a top. That and an oversized dress shirt that fell to Adrienne's knees, augmented with strategic rips and streaks of black and pink nail polish. It was a provocative look even if you didn't peg the garments as souvenirs of family annihilation, stolen from Mark and Eleanor's closets.

It was Scott, the student teacher, who first spotted him in the hallway. "You might want to do some of those buttons up."

"I actually don't, but thanks," the demon said, bypassing him.

Scott blocked Nyhiloteph's path, trying to muster some of the authority his title conferred on him but which his works hadn't earned. "That wasn't a suggestion, Adrienne." You can see your…" He gestured to the demon's chest, groping for the word *bra*. Which was almost entirely visible beneath the mesh of the camisole. Black fabric dotted with pink hearts, a pink frill lining each cup.

"My shoulders are covered," Nyhiloteph countered.

"Nothing else is."

A crowd had started to form around them, rubberneckers lingering to watch the collision. Geeks and cool kids alike, band geeks and athletes, a few of the smoking pit punks.

"You know," Nyhiloteph said, "it's not a pedagogical best practice to focus on policing what students wear rather than the course content. Youth is a time for self-discovery, and adolescents need a non-restrictive environment that encourages creativity and self-expression. Isn't the whole point of secondary education to prepare young adults for independence?"

Plagiarist bitch! I thought. I'd written that speech, years ago, read it aloud at a school board meeting, when I'd rallied my seventh grade class to protest against a trustee's school uniform proposal. I hoped it'd been plucked from Adrienne's memories, as the alternative was unsettling.

Scott went fish-mouthed, powerless against my superior rhetoric.

One of the punks piped up, "Yeah man, let her dress how she wants."

Other voices joined the chorus:

"Leave her alone, she's not hurting anyone."

"Freedom's a Charter right, you know."

"Don't be a cop."

"You used to be fun, Scott."

Scott flushed red, and when he grabbed Nyhiloteph's arm – a no-no for school staff in the current century – I was shocked the demon didn't rip his off. But his insolent smirk only brightened, the edges of Adrienne's red lips fluttering.

"We're not going to litigate this publicly," Scott declared. "We'll discuss this in my office."

Someone yelled, "You don't have an office, Scott!" To my shock, it was Chess Club Shanna, who'd never back-talked a teacher in her entire educational career.

Scott scowled, face turning from red to purple, tugging at his tie with one hand while holding onto Nyhiloteph with the other. "Don't you people have somewhere to be?"

"We know you don't," laughed the punk, golden mohawk bobbing.

Nyhiloteph defused the situation before it could ignite, clasped hands and thank-yous, sounding like a gracious political prisoner consoling supporters before being taken away. A few diehards trailed the demon as Scott marched him down the hall, but Nyhiloteph shooed them off, so in the end it was only me. I was curious because Scott truly didn't have his own office, and he was leading Nyhiloteph away from the principal's lair. It was only after the hallway emptied, even the rebels safely in class, when the mismatched pair walked arm-in-arm into a supply closet, that I realized it was Nyhiloteph leading Scott.

Chapter 26

Abdul dreamed of boats and islands. Four sailors (him, Brady, Jackson, and an alternating vision of Adrienne and myself) coming to rest on a rock in an acid sea, pressing closer and closer together as the land they stood on eroded. "How did we go from having the time of our lives to this?" dream-Abdul asked, and Jackson replied: "We'll be fine if we push someone off once it gets too small." He awoke as the stone under his feet crumbled, sending him sliding into the churning hiss.

He asked Brady to meet him for lunch the next day. They sat at a picnic table in the middle of the seniors' quad, getting spattered by rogue acorns and elm leaves. Around them, other students laughed, rustling paper bags and packages of ramen. Brady unwrapped a ham sandwich, the same mom-packed lunch he'd been eating since he was eight.

"Should we talk about...what happened?" Abdul said.

Brady shook his head. "I really don't want to talk about that ever again."

"What happened to, 'when this is all over we'll laugh about it'?"

Brady glowered. "You know I was trying to lighten the mood."

"Sorry, cheap shot." Abdul inhaled. "Listen, I don't want to re-live… that… either, but wasn't what happened after… kind of weird?"

"The Jackson and Lucy saliva exchange?"

"I wouldn't put it in those terms. But yes, that."

He turned over his milk carton to look in the spout, finding not a drop left. "I especially don't want to talk about that."

"Didn't it seem like there was something off about it?" Abdul pressed.

At the next table, someone yelled, "Delete that!" A commotion as a phone was smacked to the ground. Both boys turned their heads to watch the scuffle, grateful to look anywhere else.

"Heck yeah, it was weird, but none of our business. Like, I know he had that thing going with Adrienne, but now that she's…"

"But it wasn't Jackson who initiated the…"

"He finished it, though."

Repressing the image of Jackson sucking face, Abdul extended his arm and smacked Brady across the forehead.

"Ow!"

"Pay attention, man! Does it not seem at all weird to you that Lucy, who is not into guys, nudge nudge wink wink, initiated a steamy make-out with Jackson, who I'm pretty sure is still a male?"

Brady blinked. "What are you saying, Abdul?"

He lowered his voice to a whisper. "I'm saying, how do we know whatever you guys brought back from the woods was really her?"

Finally.

Jackson tailed Nyhiloteph around school like a puppy, and it took two days of spying and stalking until Abdul and Brady could catch him alone.

"We need to talk," the boys said simultaneously, and they sounded so much like mafia enforcers that Jackson allowed them to frogmarch him into the boys' washroom. After checking to make sure the stalls were empty, the guys stood between him and the door. Then they shuffled their feet, having thought through everything up to this moment.

It was Brady who spoke first. "We're worried about Lucy - or Adrienne, or whatever she is."

"Emphasis on that last one," added Abdul.

"Abdul, we talked about this in the car..."

"You were wrong then," Abdul said. "Whatever's going on, it's not normal, and it's not Lucy."

"I don't know what you're talking about."

"Come on. She went from murdering people to kissing you in full view of everyone. You don't think that was odd?"

Jackson blushed. "It was a stressful situation. She needed..."

Abdul cut him off. "Comfort?"

"Dude, I'm stressed all the time," Brady said. "Tongue hockey with my best friend isn't usually my soothing activity of choice."

"No, you just get high," Jackson retorted.

"That's not what this is about," Abdul said.

"Lucy's a lesbian!" Brady blurted.

Jackson's jaw dropped. "What, you have a problem with that, too?"

"I'm just saying, it's generally suspicious when a chick who likes chicks shoves her tongue down a dude's throat."

"You guys are disgusting," Jackson said, pushing past them. "Let me through."

Abdul shoved him back. "Jack, I know you're protective of her, but it's not Lucy we're talking about! Or even Adrienne. We're trying to say, there's something else inside her."

"That makes no sense at all!" Jackson replied.

"HOW HAS ANY OF THIS MADE SENSE!?" Abdul exclaimed, stopping Jackson's retreat. "This whole thing from the very beginning has been lunacy! The scary book, the pig fetus, the circle of salt. Adrienne showing up at school saying she's Lucy when she's not like Lucy at all, killing people, calling us to hide the bodies..."

"Making out with you," Brady repeated, as if he'd forgotten the first half of the conversation.

Jackson went red. "I know exactly what this is about," he exclaimed, pointing at Brady. "You're jealous because I have someone in my life and you don't. And you –" He switched his accusing finger to Abdul, sneering. "You're just worried you're going to get in trouble."

"Of course, I'm worried I'll get in trouble!" Abdul yelled back. "She had us committing crimes for her! Do you know what the sentence is for aiding-"

The bathroom door opened. The boys froze, faces turning to ash.

Nyhiloteph, as Adrienne, poked his head in. "Having fun without me?"

The demon's look today was punk chic with an Adrienne-appropriate polish: cropped vinyl motorcycle jacket over a red-and-blue striped tee, topping high-waisted skinny jeans of unfaded black. The nose ring was gone, the nostril swollen where it'd become infected, a mismatch of silver bracelets – real silver, as they'd been Eleanor's – clanged against each other on the demon's slim wrists, thick as a wrist cuff. Around Nyhiloteph's neck was the white-gold chain Adrienne had once thrown through me. His breath was rank, spreading to fill every stall.

"What are you doing here?" Abdul demanded.

"Jackson and I have class. What are you guys doing?"

"Just talking," Jackson said.

Nyhiloteph cocked his head. "About?"

No one answered.

"Alright, leave me out of the boys' club if you want. You coming, Jack?"

Brady interjected suddenly. "Why don't you come in and get him? You can't, can you? You have to be invited in, bloodsucker!"

He sounded unhinged. Abdul knew it, groaning and putting his head in his hands. Jackson just scowled.

"Brady, this is the men's room."

He walked past them without resistance, accepting Nyhiloteph's outstretched hand.

Chapter 27

Michelle's bedroom was a mess of clothes, hamper knocked askew with the weight of hastily thrown laundry. Knickknacks from various stages of life intermingled on top of her dresser, dollar store unicorns and souvenirs from family trips alongside perfume bottles and jewellery trees. Books, magazines, binders and albums strained the brackets of shelves. An antique vanity reflected the war zone back at itself.

I was in no place to judge; my bedroom had always been just as bad.

Michelle was lying on top of her duvet, math textbook open in front of her, phone propped by her ear. "I don't know how I'm gonna survive this," she was saying to the person on the other end. "I shouldn't have signed up for calculus, it's going to bring my average down like five percent."

Her arms were crossed, so I didn't see the scarred one until she stifled a yawn. Her forearm was red and swollen, almost twice its usual size, and Nyhiloteph's scratch had erupted in puss-bloated blisters, ready to burst. I couldn't fathom how she hadn't sought medical attention.

"No, Ker's been weird with me lately. I don't know what I did, but I don't think she'll let me use her notes this time."

I listened raptly to the conversation, searching for subtle notes of something not-right, little lapses that would suggest her mind was not her own, that the real Michelle had been buried under an all-consuming demonic consciousness. Mostly, though, she just talked about equations. She was trying to get into vet school and worried her math grade would sink her; there weren't many slots in Canada and she was worried she'd have to move to Europe to get her degree like one of her dad's friend's daughters had had to do. That girl had a really high average but it wasn't quite good enough, and yeah, she'd be able to practice in Canada if she got her vet degree in Ireland, but she wasn't sure she wanted to move that far…

I was starting to zone out when she got a call on her other line. Unconsciously, she scratched at her wound; the scabs opened up, sending streams of pus dripping down her arm. "I gotta go." Then: "Hi, Adrienne."

The other voice rattled the plastic of the phone. Nyhiloteph was making no attempt to do teenage girl, but Michelle didn't seem to notice.

"Hey, girlyyyy," the demon cooed. "I've been thinking about Grad Oscars."

"Me too!" Michelle enthused. "I've got so many ideas. Nalo was making these cute felt pins for all the nominees. Can you check how that's coming? She hasn't answered any of my texts.

And I know Kerri bought a bunch of those purple streamers, but they're so tacky, and I was thinking instead…"

"String the walls with your large intestine, for all I care. My only concern is with the ceremony."

"Of course," Michelle said, nodding obsequiously. "What's on your mind?"

"I was thinking about a special award. To recognize all the hardships people have overcome this year."

"I don't know," Michelle replied, rolling onto her back. "Grad Oscars is supposed to be fun. If you ask me, we're already pushing it with the tribute to the dead girl."

Nice.

"I can assure you," Nyhiloteph replied, "this will make it much more fun."

"It's your show, Adrienne," Michelle replied, a blank look coming into her eye. "Just tell me how I can make it happen."

"I need you to help me find names of nominees," the demon said. "We both know I don't know who any of these losers are."

Michelle cast an eye across her mess. "I can dig out last year's yearbook, I guess."

"Do that."

They poured over that book for an hour, trying to identify people through old class photos, with Nyhiloteph feeding Michelle clues like "chess club girl" and "guy with the bad hair who smokes." I couldn't understand why he didn't just ask Adrienne, unless he feared he would lose his hold on her if she understood the full extent of his plan.

When they hung up, Michelle rolled back into her previous position, but looked unsettled. It was four and a half minutes before she moved again, her expression blank as she slid open the vanity drawer and withdrew a pair of scissors.

"Oh no," I gasped.

Michelle pulled out the chair and sat down, lifting the hem of her shirt. Raising the scissors above her navel, she pointed the sharpest blade downward and drove it into her stomach.

(String the walls with your large intestine, for all I care)

She screamed, not expecting that level of pain, digging the scissor blade deeper into her gut. A geyser of blood formed around her hand and she jerked the blade to the left, opening a longer gash. Her eyes rolled into the back of her head, but she kept pushing, slicing layers of flesh and muscle until the wound almost reached her left thigh. When it was wide enough, she dropped the scissors onto the surface of the vanity, then inserted her hand between the slashed flaps of skin, feeling around for a coil to grab onto.

I forgot myself and flew shrieking from the room, calling for her parents to save her. Of course, no one heard me.

Chapter 28

"She sliced open her own stomach?" Artemis asked.

I nodded. "I guess she took Nyhiloteph literally."

"Ugggh," he said.

"I know," I said.

"Is she okay?" he asked.

"I don't know, I left."

"I'm guessing she won't be on the decorating committee, now."

I snickered, feeling bad but not that bad.

"Why don't I feel very much about any of this?" I asked him. "Shouldn't I be freaking out, inconsolable with remorse, something?"

He shrugged. "I don't know. Maybe the dead have perspective. The worst thing that can happen to us already has."

I shook my head. "Watching what Nyhiloteph is doing to my friends is a whole lot worse than dying in that crash. I should be crushed."

"Well, technically, you were."

Fuck, that was funny. I suppressed my laugh because I wanted to have a serious conversation, and Artemis took any opportunity to be avoidant. I said nothing and watched him expectantly.

"If you want my actual theory," he mused, "I think we can't feel any emotion we didn't experience in life. You never had anything that devastating happen to you when you were alive, so you're processing this at a much lower level."

"I resent that."

"You know I'm right," he said. "Think back, what was the worst thing that ever happened to you before you died?"

"I don't have to share that with you."

"You're only saying that because you can't think of something."

I couldn't argue.

"I'll fill in the blanks," he said. "Maybe a friend deserted you, and you spent a night crying because you didn't know who'd let you sit with them at lunch the next day. Maybe a relative who you didn't know well died and you got a little misty at the funeral. Perhaps you looked at someone else's paper during a test and felt guilty about it for a few months after. That all probably felt awful when it happened, but not accidentally-caused-the-deaths-of-several-people awful. But those mild griefs represent the upper limit - or I should say, the lower limit - of how bad you can feel now."

I gritted my ghost-teeth. "I will begrudgingly admit that makes sense."

"Don't begrudge me anything. You should be grateful you haven't been a wreck this whole time."

I thought of Artemis's deep sorrow the day I'd found him in the attic, and wondered which of his earthly sufferings had equaled that. Based on what I'd seen of his mom, he'd had no shortage.

"Your buddy there's fucked, eh?" he observed, with the utmost tact.

"I know!" I snapped. "Have you made any progress on the exorcism thing?"

A flutter of a smile. "I was about to tell you when you came in, but I couldn't get a word in edgewise."

"Artemis!" I smacked him.

He opened the massive yet fragile book on his desk, plunging his finger at a set of inky Latin phrases. "I have identified the exorcism rite that will likely evict Nyhiloteph," he announced, extending his other arm in a flourish.

"Woo!" I cheered. "I wish I could buy you a drink."

"There's a complication," he warned.

"Fuck, what now?"

"We obviously can't do it, because we're dead. We'll need to find a human we can communicate with and convince them to do it." He raised his pointer finger. "And not my fucking mother."

As if on cue, someone pounded on the door. "Wouldn't it be weird if it was your mom again?" I asked.

"Don't even joke."

I rolled my eyes and went to the window, finding two young men on the stoop. "It's even worse," I called. "My friends are here."

"All of them?"

"Just Abdul and Brady."

Abdul was politely banging on the glass. "Sir, are you open?" he called. "Your posted hours say…"

"Fuck this," Brady muttered.

I heard a grunt, then Abdul's muffled voice. "What are you gonna do?"

"What is he going to do?" Artemis echoed.

I floated to the window and pressed my face to the glass. Brady was struggling to unearth a large rock, embedded where the garden used to be.

"Oh, fuck!" I yelled.

"This guy knows what's going on with our friends," Brady declared, brandishing the stone threateningly. "And we're not leaving until he tells us."

"Not necessarily!" Abdul cried, waving his arms. "It was a hunch!"

I jumped back from the window as the rock flew through it. Glass exploded inward, drowning out the sound of Abdul shrieking: "This is breaking and entering!"

"We're just here to ask questions," Brady said, as if that were a legal defence. Shards crunched under his feet as he climbed the stairs and reached through the opening in the window, bending his forearm at a weird angle to grope for the lock. He drew back as glass sliced his wrist.

"In retrospect, we could have just let him in," Artemis mused.

"Really?" I asked, cocking my head toward the rotting corpse on the floor.

"Forgot about that."

Brady's fingers grasped the lock. He pushed his body closer to the window to get a better hold, stretched, and flicked it, looking back to see if Abdul was still with him. "If we stop now, it's only vandalism," Abdul advised. Brady pushed the door open.

Abdul sighed. "Great, good show."

The bickering stopped when their eyes fell on the bloody heap on the floor.

Part III:

Two Outta Three Ain't Bad

Chapter 29

OTTAWA: Police are investigating after the owner of an occult store was found dead Monday.

The body of 31-year-old Arthur "Artemis" McLuhan was discovered in a new age bookshop in the west end, with injuries described as "severe blunt force trauma."

Police say he was dead for several weeks before being found by two teenagers, who said they suspected something was amiss after finding the shop locked with lights on during business hours.

"It just seemed like something was off, you know?" said Brady Thomas, who forced the door after glimpsing McLuhan's body through the front window.

McLuhan had no criminal history and was described as a loner by those who knew him. "He didn't really seem to have anything going on in his life," a neighbour told reporters. "Certainly not anything that would make someone do this."

Anyone with information is asked to call...

Artemis slammed the big book shut the moment the cop touched it.

"Ow!" the officer shouted, snatching back his hand. The patch on his uniform read METZ.

His partner, ATWELL, was examining a terrarium containing a lifelike infant skull. "What's up?"

"This book just shut by itself," Metz said, nursing his fingers.

"Don't tell me you're getting spooked, Metz. Contrary to what everything in here says, there's no such thing as ghosts."

Hovering over Atwell's shoulder, Artemis knocked the terrarium out of his hands. Atwell jumped, his eyes wide as the circumference of the shattering glass. The skull rolled across the wood without cracking.

"Don't be churlish," I chided.

"We can't have them messing around here," Artemis shot back. "We still need these books. And because they think I'm some sort of chicken-sacrificing occultist murdered by a rival magician, everything in here could be considered evidence."

Artemis had fanciful ideas about what the cops suspected regarding his death, but I didn't want to ruin his fun.

Evidence bag in hand, Metz went for the book again, this time with a set of tongs. It slipped from their grip, impact rattling the tabletop. When he tried again, and Artemis pushed the book an inch out of his reach.

The cop lowered the tongs. "Are you seeing this?"

But Atwell was pre-occupied, flipping through a paperback that had caught his eye. It had an oil painting of a nude woman on the cover, and he was flipping through the other illustrations. I saw him lick his finger to flip the page.

"Gross," I muttered. Figuring he deserved a shock, I fiddled with the bracket of the nearest shelf. It collapsed. Atwell threw the naked witch book as he scrambled out of the way.

Artemis scowled. "Didn't we just discuss the importance of keeping my store in good working order?"

I looked at him innocently. "Artemis, the guy licked his finger to turn a page. He probably bends the spines and folds the corners to mark his place."

Artemis forgot himself and bent to sweep up the fallen books. He froze midway through the act as he locked eyes with Atwell, who gaped in horror at what he saw as a set of magic books floating of their own accord.

Both cops were gone in seconds.

Chapter 30

Window cranked and screen popped, Brady stuck out his head to feel the fresh evening air. He wasn't supposed to be smoking in the house, wasn't supposed to be smoking at all, but it was an open secret that he did. His parents pretended they didn't know because they didn't really care, but stopped short of wanting to condone it. And anyway, after what he'd seen, they couldn't possibly begrudge him.

Brady flopped onto the bed, bouncing slightly as his back hit the mattress, and lay back with his hands behind his head. I was watching him from the upper corner of the room, clinging to the ceiling like a spiderweb, when hazy gaze landed on my patch of wall. His brow furrowed. "Luce? Is that you?"

Artemis either didn't believe me or didn't care when I told him my good luck.

"Wait a minute, I thought he's been high in your presence before? You said he was when they dumped Adrienne's parents."

"Yeah, that confused me too," I admitted. "Maybe it varies by the strain. I asked him what he was smoking and he said it was called 'Screaming Goat.'"

Artemis rubbed his temples. "I feel like I'm in a Cheech and Chong horror movie."

"Artemis, this is the first lucky break we've had in weeks."

"A turning point indeed. Your dumbest friend can see you, but only when he's fried on goat. This is truly the end of the beginning."

"Do you have any better ideas?"

He shrugged. "Maybe haunt that Abdul a bit, get him on board. From your account, he's the only one of you who has a lick of sense."

"I tried to haunt Adrienne and it made things worse." I pondered options, then shook my head. "Do you think we can get that book to Brady?"

"Which book?" he asked.

"The one you've been studying?" I said. "With the instructions for the exorcism?"

Artemis glanced at the tome sitting open on his desk. It was half a foot thick, bound in threadbare leather that peeled and flaked. The pages were thick but brittle, threatening to snap with careless handling. Perhaps only a ghost had a touch gentle enough.

"Oh no, this is a reference book," he declared, like it was the most obvious thing in the world. "It doesn't say anything about how to do the ritual."

My jaw dropped. "Then what the fuck does it do?"

"It provides a list of types of rituals that work on particular sub-classes of demon. You see, first I had to determine what type of demon Nyhiloteph is. Then I was able to consult this book to find the proper rite."

I blinked. "Please tell me you actually have a book that actually explains how to do the ritual."

"That I do," Artemis said, pulling open a drawer and withdrawing, with a flourish, a little black volume barely thicker than a magazine. In small white writing, the cover read: *Secular Exorcisms: Simplified Rites for Every Situation.*

The medium grinned. "As your bud there might say, 'Chillax, bro.'"

Abdul's sole vice was online strategy gaming, so he was wide awake spreading blight through a fledgling city-state's stores of corn when Brady called. Abdul groaned. Brady was the last person he wanted to hear from; he wasn't convinced they weren't both going to get arrested for the gong show at the bookstore. Then, of course, the police would match Brady's fingerprints to something at Adrienne's house, or they'd get DNA from his pile of vomit, and they'd all go down for triple murder.

He let the phone ring out, only for Brady to call back. He was oddly persistent tonight. Usually if Abdul didn't answer on the first try, he'd get impatient and find someone else to call.

There was a knock on the wall from the next room. His mother had an almost supernatural sensitivity to phone vibrations;

she claimed they shook the whole house. "Either pick it up or shut it off," she yelled, voice muffled between layers of insulation.

"Sorry," Abdul called back, sliding his finger across the phone screen.

Brady's stoner-boy drawl grated. "Man, you're not gonna believe what happened."

"Why are you calling me, then?"

"Because it's important. Lucy's here."

Abdul stiffened. "What?"

"Not like, Adrienne-Lucy," Brady clarified. "The ghosty Lucy. She says-"

"Brady, are you high?"

"I have to be. Or else I can't see her."

Abdul generally hung up on Brady when he called with weed-infused ramblings, but the apparent hallucination had him worried. "To clarify - our dead friend who is currently possessing the body of Jackson's girlfriend came to you as a ghost and is... telling you to do things?"

"Nooo," Brady replied. "Well, she told me to call you, so I guess she's sort of telling me to do things. Oh, and she wants us to go to the store and get this exercise book."

I would have corrected him to "exorcism book" but I didn't think it would make anything better. Brady'd blown it.

Not that he wasn't still trying. "Listen, it's hard to explain. You have to come over to my house right now and smoke some Screaming Goat..."

"Screaming what?!" Abdul breathed deeply as Brady unhelpfully explained the differences between various weed strains. "Brady, come on. I'm not going to smoke marijuana with you. Who do you think you're talking to?"

"I don't want you to smoke weed with me - I mean, it might help you relax a bit, but..."

Abdul hung up. He rubbed his temples and turned back to his game, the convulsions of starving villagers reflected in his blue light glasses.

"Can Brady slip something in his drink?" Artemis suggested, and it honestly wasn't his worst idea.

Chapter 31

I visited Abdul during his spare period, when I knew he'd be alone in the science lab.

I had a full script that I'd planned to write out, both to explain the situation and prove my ghostly existence. Except when I lifted the piece of chalk and pressed it to the board, my hand started to shake. Fuck. I re-calibrated, thought of something simpler to write. What had I said to Adrienne? This is Lucy. When I thought of writing that, my hand steadied. But "This is Lucy" hadn't been helpful at all. I considered "This is Lucy. Listen to Brady." My hand seized up and the chalk fell and broke on the floor.

I ran through a dozen alternatives. Everything I was allowed to write was ominous or vaguely threatening. Anything with any specificity was automatically rejected. "You are doomed" worked but "You are in danger" did not. I could write Adrienne's name but not advise Abdul to avoid her. Finally, I just erased everything because scaring Abdul into a heart attack would leave me no further ahead.

My problem this whole time, I realized, was that I'd been trying to act like a person. Helping my friends, trying to talk to people rationally – these were all things living people did, which I wasn't allowed to do because I was dead. That was why everything I'd done thus far had gone horribly wrong. I was a ghost and I needed to do ghost shit.

Rows of fluorescents sputtered to life as Abdul entered the darkened lab. Sinks and taps lined one wall, glinting like medical instruments laid out on a table. Ever safety-conscious, he made for the drawer where goggles and safety equipment were stored, just as the lights flicked off. Abdul turned, checking for someone coming in behind him. There was no one.

No one but me.

Abdul doubled back, flicking the switch again.

As he selected a pair of safety goggles, I cracked the glass in both lenses. I did the same for the second set he reached for. Some sort of air pressure change, he thought, waiting a minute and trying for a third pair. This time I let him pick up the glasses before snapping them in his hand. He closed the drawer. I sprinted across the room to kill the lights again.

I was having too much fun with this. But I hadn't gone far enough - he could still blame natural phenomena. It would be a stretch, but nothing I'd done justified him in concluding that his dead friend who was supposedly possessing a live friend was visiting him as a ghost to recruit him into a supernatural war. That was admittedly a tall order.

I scanned the room for an object I could do something spooky with, wishing there were still pig fetuses lying around. I found something even better.

Abdul had just turned away from the light switch when a grinning display skeleton came careening toward him, rattling on its wheeled stand. It came to an anti-climactic stop three feet away, plastic bones clacking together.

"Very funny, Brady," he called. "Come out now, you shouldn't be fooling around in a room full of chemicals."

I had him facing the right direction now, and it was time for my grand finale.

Abdul's chin flicked up to see one of the ceiling tiles being moved out of its bracket. Moved by me. As I pushed the tile out of place, a thin black book fell out of the widening crack. It fluttered gracefully and landed, face-up, on the counter that would have been Abdul's workstation.

Abdul's first response was to flee. I'd predicted that. The tile clattered to the ground as I discarded it and raced him to the door. I slammed it shut just as he put his hand on the knob.

This is where the blackboard came in handy. Catching Abdul's attention with a loud tap of the chalk on the board, I wrote one of the pre-approved words in my classic shitty ghost scrawl: LOOK.

Abdul's legs shook so badly that his walk to the counter was a Frankenstein lurch, like his body was revolting against him. He came just close enough to lean over and read the title: *Secular Exorcisms: Simplified Rites for Every Situation.*

"Now I know this is Brady!" he yelled, rearing back. "Or Adrienne, or someone!" I rolled my eyes. As if Brady could have accomplished this - I'd barely managed it. Erasing the board, I wrote: NO IT'S NOT, then strode across the room to open the book. Abdul's jaw dropped as the book flew open of its own accord, pages flipping rapidly until they stopped at our ritual.

Propping it open at the correct section, I returned to the chalkboard and wrote: Believe me yet?

Artemis' record player had been left undisturbed, so I pressed play on whatever was in it and did a little twirl to the music. The dance didn't actually work, because it turned out to be a grunge record, but I was so happy it didn't matter. For the first time in weeks, things were falling into place.

"I'm guessing your smart friend is on board?" Artemis asked, looking up from his book in the corner of the room. He was reading for pleasure today, one of those seventies Lovecraft paperbacks with black jackets and psychedelic faces staring out from the cover.

"Abdul is in! He was just getting off the phone with Brady when I left."

Artemis smiled wanly.

"It is bad that I think this might work out?" I asked.

"Sometimes things work out," he said. I knew he was holding back on me. Oh well I'd give myself this one night to celebrate.

I could not give myself this one night.

Mind racing, I took leave of the store and crept into Abdul's house to consult the book under his bed. In my haste to get it to Abdul, I hadn't actually taken the time to read it myself.

It was short – 121 pages. I didn't understand how the ritual book could be so short when the reference book rivalled the vertical height of a Subway sandwich. The font wasn't even that small.

That didn't mean anything, I reasoned. After all, *Secular Exorcisms* didn't proport to contain every exorcism ritual in existence, but Artemis had assured me it had ours.

I flipped to that rite now, to the business card Artemis had inserted to mark the page. The store's name in a creepy font, above an angular doodle of a skull. I wondered if Artemis, he of the wolf shirts and the Meat Loaf worship, had designed it. It certainly didn't look like a "Madame Jade" creation.

I was procrastinating. I needed to know what Brady and Abdul were in for, but I didn't want to know. Abdul stirred, spurring me. I didn't want to be there when he woke up; even after everything he'd already accepted, waking up to a floating book would probably scare the crap out of him.

My dead eyes well-accustomed to the dark, I started reading.

Artemis dropped headfirst to the floor when I shook him awake.

(Yes – ghosts sleep. No, they do not generally sleep hanging upside down like bats. Artemis finds he can only drift off with both feet firmly planted on the ceiling, "swaying as if in the womb," but that is far from normal. Artemis is a weird guy.)

"Did you know that to do the exorcism, they need to capture her physically?" I yelled as he sat up, rubbing the back of his head even though it couldn't possibly be hurting.

"How else the fuck do you think an exorcism is performed?" he asked. "Have you not seen *The Exorcist*?"

"I didn't think it was like the movies," I admitted. "Nothing else is."

"William Peter Blatty knew his shit." He stood up, brushing non-existent dust off his pants, an old mannerism he'd held onto. "Now that we're on the subject - something else I wanted to eventually bring up."

"What?" I asked, heart sinking. These late-in-the-game Artemis reveals were never good.

"Since they need Nyhiloteph in their possession anyway, you may want to suggest that instead of attempting a risky and potentially unsuccessful exorcism, they might want to…" He made a clicking sound with his tongue and did a stabby gesture with his right hand.

"No way."

"Most foolproof way to get rid of a demon is to kill the host. And it would be best to do it now before Nyhil finishes consuming her."

"I'm not asking my friends to kill someone."

"You're already asking them to kidnap someone."

Fuck.

"That'll be an incredibly hard sell," I reasoned. "I don't even know if they'll want to kidnap her, once they realize that's what they have to do."

"I know. Just...throwing it out there."

I sighed. "Am I deluding myself, Artemis? Is there any chance that this actually works, or am I just going to get my friends thrown in jail?"

Artemis sat on the edge of his desk, turned his head to follow the glare of the moon through the bay window. "I don't know, Lucy. I honestly don't. There's a reason I didn't want to get involved in any of this shit while I was alive. If they're going to have any chance of making this work, they'll need an airtight plan and they'll have to execute it perfectly."

"We're getting together tomorrow to figure that out. Brady's going to smoke the Goat so he can translate for me."

"That's good," Artemis said.

"I'm not leaving them to their own devices on this," I assured him.

Little did I know.

Chapter 32

Abdul pressed close to the hot metal wall of a portable classroom, watching and waiting. He was dressed as inconspicuously as he could without attracting attention, jeans and a hoodie, hood up. The hoodie, unfortunately, said "Tom Thomson Science Olympians" on the front, so he wouldn't be difficult to identify. A dishrag, soaked in chloroform, was wedged under his sleeve.

On days the demon had English for first period, he would enter through the double doors at the far end of the school. There was generally a bottleneck in the mornings when the first crush of students entered, and Nyhiloteph – who relished walking into class late – was usually the last to enter. He tended to spend this time ambling along the outskirts of the crowd, observing and eavesdropping from a distance; he reminded me of a wolf I'd once seen in a zoo, who spent its days circling the perimeter of its enclosure, searching for weak spots in the fence.

Abdul and Brady were betting on Nyhiloteph himself being the weak spot. If Abdul approached casually enough, they reasoned, they might be able to chloroform him before he caught on, and escape the notice of the preoccupied crowd.

This scheme was on the same level as men who hire hitmen to kill their wives and pay through joint bank accounts, or drug dealers who call the cops when clients slip them fake bills. That is to say, not what I would've done. Originally, the three of us were supposed to hash out a strategy together, Brady interpreting through a fog of Screaming Goat. What ensued instead was a comedy of errors. The day we were set to confer, Brady failed a French test so abysmally that Madame Hanson called his parents, who responded by raiding his bedroom, smashing his pipe, and flushing his entire stash down the toilet. Grounded, Brady frantically texted a smoker's pit friend to see if he could pick up another eighth of Screaming Goat for him. The friend went to the head shop and said no dice, Screaming Goat had been discontinued (wonder why). Instead, he'd picked up Brady a pre-roll of what the store-owner assured him was "the next best thing." Brady told him "Thanks, drop it off to Abdul," much to Abdul's discomfort.

Abdul was allowed into the Thomas house only because he could credibly claim he was there to work on a group project (which was technically true). He was the last person Brady's parents would have suspected of smuggling in drugs. "Never make me do this again," he'd ordered, tossing the baggie onto Brady's bedspread.

"The next best thing" was no Screaming Goat. I never appeared to him, could only helplessly listen in as they threw out increasingly bad ideas. I tried to make my presence known, at times, throwing things and banging on walls when I thought they were being particularly stupid. They thought the banging meant I agreed with them.

So, there we were.

Brady waited by the rear gate, half a block from his house which was unlocked and arranged for the ritual. Chairs and tables pushed aside, every ounce of salt in his cupboard poured out to form a five-pointed star on the carpet, large enough in the centre to fit a teen girl. The demon would be sealed within the star; all they needed to do at that point was say the words I'd circled in the book – the complete exorcism rite, followed by an incantation to bind the demon. The latter was Artemis's solution to the problem of an angry spirit on the loose; immediately after the expulsion, they would have to direct Nyhiloteph into an empty vessel, where he would be trapped permanently (unless, of course, someone made the mistake of letting him out). Any container would do, the text assured us. Brady had chosen a cylindrical Pringles can for the honour.

There was a lot that could go wrong with this plan, but ironically, none of my fears came to fruition. The complication that revealed itself was that today, Nyhiloteph was not dead last in line. Michelle in her new wheelchair lagged behind, strategically keeping her master in her line of sight. Watching from the shadow of the portables, Abdul twitched, his muscles debating whether to go or not. He could outrun the wheelchair, but if Michelle screamed, he'd be swarmed.

"Don't risk it," I said, wishing he could hear.

The chair dipped as Michelle wheeled into a tire track, the aftermath of some sloppy driver veering onto the grass. She jiggled the wheels, found herself stuck, and started to get up to dislodge the chair. "Whoa!" someone called, and Ben Choi rushed over to help her. "Don't hurt yourself."

"It's okay," Michelle insisted, but Ben was righting the chair and taking the liberty of pushing her toward the door. "Seriously, let me go," she snapped, as they overtook Nyhiloteph.

Abdul made a break for the demon. My heart sank.

Instead of ambling up casually, clapping Nyhiloteph on the shoulder as old friends do and surprising him with the sedative, Abdul, nervous, ran. Nyhiloteph didn't turn at the sound of pounding feet, but Michelle did. She wrenched herself from the wheelchair, screaming as her stitches ripped, and rushed Abdul with outstretched fingers.

Ben stood flabbergasted, still holding the chair.

Michelle caught air before pinning Abdul to the ground. A dump of red blood stained his lap as Michelle's wound re-opened into a geyser gush.

"Gahhh!"

He swung his rag-hand towards Michelle's face, but she caught him by the forearm and bent it backward. Abdul's arm snapped.

Birds flew off the telephone wires three blocks away. I'd never heard anyone scream that loudly. Michelle had broken Abdul's elbow, not just broken it but severed it, reduced his arm to a stump with a jagged branch of bone sticking out.

"Holy shit!"

"What the fuck?"

Now people were paying attention, though no one had the presence of mind to do anything. Nyhiloteph covered his mouth with his hand, hiding his pleasure under a façade of shock.

The wound in Michelle's stomach was growing as she knelt on all fours, her innards pushing up against the straining stitches. If she noticed she didn't care, as she wasn't done with Abdul. Raking her claws down his face, she went for his eyes; when he shielded them with his good hand, she switched tactics, shoving her fingers into his mouth to force his jaw open. Like she was trying to tear him apart from the inside. Abdul bit down and she punched him, fist smashing his cheekbone. His mouth popped open. A second hand widened the gap, forcing his chin down until it was flush with his throat.

Brady slammed into Michelle just before Abdul's jaw broke. A trail of blood tracked her path as she stumbled and fell. I cringed when she landed on her stomach.

Abdul was still on his back, making little gasping sounds that threatened to crest into screams. Brady clung to his side, coaxing him to sit up. Abdul's eyes were glued to his ruined arm. As teachers swooped in too fucking late to do anything, Brady surreptitiously picked up the rag and shoved it into his pocket. No one noticed, and Brady got away with the incriminating evidence. It was the smartest move he'd made all month.

Chapter 33

A network of IV cords snaked around a metal stand at the head of the bed, the kind that people in movies always detach themselves from without asking whether they still need the fluids. Abdul was awake, but out-of-it, Brady asleep in the chair next to him.

Abdul must have been on enough painkillers to access the Screaming Goat plane, because he blinked when I came into the room. "Lucy?"

"That's my name."

"Really?"

"Yes. It's really me."

"I'm sorry," he said.

I wanted to apologize back, tell him how wrong it was that he'd been forced to clean up my mess, but I could tell he wasn't at peak processing power. "It's okay," I settled. "I'm sorry, too."

Brady snored loudly. Abdul started like he was just noticing him for the first time, scowling when he saw Brady drooling all over the chair-back.

I realized I should leave. This was a place for the living.

"Goodbye, Abdul."

"Wait!" he cried, slightly more lucid. "What now?"

We didn't have much time. I would be invisible to him once the drugs wore off. "Nothing, Abdul. There's nothing you can do. Just stay out of Adrienne's way and you'll be safe."

"But-"

I cut him off and tried to speak commandingly, wishing I had that authoritative tone that Nyhiloteph did, that made people do whatever he wanted. "Don't try anything again. There is no chance at success. What's going to happen is going to happen. Stay away."

Brady snorted, stirred, and woke, eyes darting as he tried to remember where he was. "Abby!" he exclaimed, slapping Abdul's shoulder affectionately. Abdul flinched and cried out; it was his broken arm. "Sorry, man."

I slipped out the door when they weren't looking, laughing despite everything. I would miss those guys.

On my way out I passed a private room that had the name "McLuhan" written on the door. The thin man in the bed saw me and made eye contact. I nodded and passed him by. I wondered if I should have said something to him, for his son who wanted to visit and couldn't, but I didn't. I'm not sure if that was the right decision, but it was the most likely to do no further harm.

I was standing by the elevator - out of habit - when the doors slid open to reveal Jackson, who whipped out of the elevator and ran down the hall like a nurse rushing to a flatliner. He barged into Abdul's room without knocking, didn't inquire as to his welfare before yelling, "What do you think you're doing?"

Brady rose in his chair. "Uhh, talking to my friend who lost an arm?"

"Don't give me that. Lucy saw you guys, she said you were following her."

Brady forced a laugh. "Whatever she's smoking, I want some."

He was so unprepared for Jackson's fist, he didn't even try to block it. Brady reeled sideways, careening into the IV pole. Abdul screeched as the cord was yanked from his wrist, spitting saline solution onto the linoleum.

"Dude, what the fuck?"

Jackson just stared at his still closed fist, as if it had acted on its own will.

Part IV:

All Revved Up With No Place to Go

Chapter 34

Abdul's first day back in class, he absent-mindedly raised his stump-arm to answer a question. Carter Daniels, sitting very close to Kerri, snickered. In retaliation, I swept the case off his desk, sending pencils and protractors scattering across the floor. If he laughed again, I'd stab him with a pen. Or maybe the pointy end of the protractor.

This was what I'd been reduced to in the days since my massive failure. Hanging around a school I no longer attended like Matthew McConaughey in *Dazed and Confused*. Artemis had urged me to try to "move on," and I had tried, but I couldn't. So here I was.

Right here, today, was especially painful. Abdul's math class technically had double the required adult supervision, but neither of these adults were adept at controlling the classroom. The teacher was a youngish, soft-spoken woman unfortunately named Ms. Biggins- colloquially known as Ms. BigTits. It had always been a running joke that all the straight guys lusted after her, but having never had a thing for teachers I'd never before realized how serious they were. Sitting in their midst in my hyper-sensitive state felt like being prodded with a dozen upright pricks. And the student teacher, stationed in here as part of his teacher's college certification, was no better than the teenagers.

The would-be-Mr. Anderson (some of the girls still called him "Scott") was seated near the door, degradingly confined to one of the half-desks the students used, when Ms. Biggins dropped a piece of chalk. She followed it across the room until it came to a stop by her mentee's seat; they bent down to pick it up at the exact same time, giving the student teacher a privileged view down her shirt. His jeans swelled, and a black spot appeared on his crotch. His face screwed up in confusion and then pain; yelping like he'd been burned, he shot out of his chair with such force that the desk toppled.

"Scott, is everything okay?" Ms. Biggins asked. He opened his mouth to give an excuse that turned into a shriek and bolted out the door.

I followed him into the nearest washroom, where he didn't bother stepping into a stall before peeling off his khakis. His briefs were soaked through with a molasses-thick black liquid; they shredded easily when he tore them off, the fabric disintegrated.

A stall door opened. Behind it was Paul Sharma, zipping his fly, his hand freezing halfway up as he took in the pants-less nightmare. "Are you oh-"

"Get out!" the aspiring educator screamed.

Paul had the wherewithal to make the sink before he complied, squirting soap and water onto his palms. "I'll call the nurse for you!" he promised, lathering as he fled into the hallway.

Alone now, Scott Anderson bounded into the nearest stall, pulling the toilet paper dispenser off the wall in his haste to get at the roll. He tried to wipe off the gunk but yanked his hand away; the seepage hurt to touch, even though five layers of tissue. The smell of it was putrid, sulphurous.

A knock on the outer door. Scott slammed against one stall wall then the other.

"What's going on in there?"

Scott didn't seem to hear the nurse, hopping to the counter as fast as he could with his pants around his ankles. Kicking them off, he straddled the sink and turned on the tap.

The nurse burst in just in time to see Scott sighing with relief, cold water washing over him beneath a cloud of black steam.

Chapter 35

"The student teacher, can you believe it?"

"I can," Artemis said. "Nothing this bHszzstard does surphxxxxxmmzz me anymore."

I didn't have the heart to tell him he was cutting out again. It had been happening a lot ever since the movers had started to clear out the store. The first time, I thought he was just trying to get out of a boring conversation; that Pee-wee Herman "you're breaking up, I can't hear you" trick. But he didn't even realize it was happening.

Previously, The Grimoire had been creepy in a homey way. Now, it was just desolate. The shelves, previously overcapacity with books, were now half empty, their contents shipped to police evidence lockers or thrift stores or landfills. The front room was filled with boxes of others to be moved. The skulls that had once glowered from wall shelves had also been taken for "analysis." A big FOR SALE sign blocked part of the bay window, a grimly funny addition to the POLICE LINE – DO NOT CROSS tape.

Artemis flickered as he approached a shelf, flipped through the handful of remaining books, then returned to his desk without withdrawing anything. His motions were jerky, like someone walking past a strobe light. He groaned as feet thumped up the steps. Muffled voices funnelled in, Metz and Atwell again. I watched Artemis closely, wondering if he would do anything to scare them away.

He met my eyes wearily. "We knew they'd be back."

"I thought you spooked them pretty good last time."

"Them or someone like them," he corrected. "It's inevitavrzrrr."

Panic flared inside me. I didn't know if Artemis could weather another box load of books being removed. This store was the only earthly thing holding him here, and I wasn't ready to be alone.

The cops were bitching as their keys clattered in the lock. "They better be ready with backup as soon as we call," Metz muttered. "With our luck the killer's hiding down there."

"Laughing at us," Atwell agreed. "We should get danger pay."

The whole story clicked into my head. The crime scene team had failed to notice the door to a basement hidden behind a drape, an omission discovered when someone else at the precinct was reviewing the blueprints. Metz and Atwell were the lucky couple dispatched to search the place.

Oh well, at least they wouldn't be messing around on the main floor.

"Keystone cops," Artemis muttered.

Neither seemed particularly eager to be here at all, and they literally did rock-paper-scissors to determine who would lead the way downstairs. Metz lost. After some more argument, he sulked across the store and pulled down the decorative curtain next to the old séance room, revealing a narrow door that gave way to a wooden staircase leading into darkness. He took the first step gingerly, flashlight beam preceding him. Atwell, anxious to meet whatever might await, followed two steps at a time, the impact of his feet straining the planks. It was interesting how differently their fears manifested, even as they both dreaded the same thing: a killer hiding in the shadows. If only they'd known two ghosts were following behind them.

Metz's flashlight beam glinted off dark glass that glowed scarlet. An iron wine rack that took up most of the back wall, rows of reds of an unknown vintage.

Atwell chuckled. "Looks like someone had a problem."

Behind me, Artemis harrumphed.

Metz approached the bottles and ran a finger along the glass, scraping off a thick layer of dust. "Couldn't have been that big of a problem. These have been here for ages."

"Not a red fan?" I asked Artemis.

"They were hers."

"Oh."

Artemis winced as Atwell removed a bottle and held it to his ear, the liquid swishing as he shook it. "Think it's still good?"

"You got an opener?" Metz replied, only half joking.

I shook my head. "How gross is that? Stealing murder victim wine."

"I used to raid my parents' liquor cabinet when I was a kid," Artemis mused. "Mix the wine and rum and vodka to make 'fruit punch.'"

"Is that why they kicked you out?"

"Fuck off, you." Artemis flickered, was more substantial for a second. Proof the man thrived on spite.

He used his burst of strength to knock the bottle from the cop's hand. It fell in slow motion and smashed in hyperspeed, glass and wine exploding across the floor. I flinched out of habit, jumping even quicker than the cops. Artemis didn't move, a look of frozen horror taking over his face.

The wine didn't settle on the floor, but gathered itself and became airborne, a floating whirlpool of dust and liquid. The gushing mass stretched to the ceiling, forming a rippling, wrinkled face and wild tendrils of hair. The head narrowed into a slim neck that spread into a waterfall, the gossamer wisps of a dress. The face – if it could be called that – opened to form a yawning chasm, and the spectre spoke. The voice was weathered and watery, like an old sea captain surfacing from a drowning to croak out one last command: *GET OUT OF MY WINE CELLAR.*

The cops didn't have to be told twice. The alcoholic spirit watched them jostle to be first up the stairs, bottlenecking at the entrance and collapsing as they broke through at the same time. Then she turned to us and said, "Not you, Artie."

"It's funny, what we imprint on," Madame Jade mused, summoning a pair of glasses from a cabinet and filling them from the tip of her index finger. "I wanted to come back to you, Artie, but every time I tried, I resurfaced inside that damned bottle. I never thought I had a booze problem before."

"No, you didn't have a problem," Artemis said ironically. He held the wine glass experimentally to his lips, wondering if he could imbibe.

"Try it!" she nudged, and Artemis tipped the glass. The liquid fell through him and spilled on the floor. Jade cackled. I set my glass down. I didn't feel like drinking anyway.

"So, kids," Jade said, crossing her legs and floating. "Tell me about the trouble you've gotten into."

Jade listened patiently, until the story of Abdul gave her pause. "So, why were you under the impression that the boys had to capture the demon?"

I turned to Artemis, whose face had fallen several inches. "Yes, why was that?"

Artemis was stumped. "I figured...well, you have to get the demon within the star of salt."

Jade frowned. "My dear, that enclosure can be as large as you want. You could have encircled the demon before he even knew it."

Artemis looked so crestfallen that all of my anger fled. Jade brought her hands together. "Well, now we know, we can move forward accordingly."

"So, to clarify," I said, "are you saying that we could, like, make a star around the perimeter of Adrienne's house?"

""The trick is doing it undetected," Jade confirmed. "And someone would have to get up close to usher the demon into the vessel, once the formalities were done."

"And that's the issue," Artemis said, defensive. "If he'd caught us in the act, before the circle was completed, we would have been fucked. And by 'us' I mean your human friends."

"Hate to break it to you, Artie -" I said.

"You don't get to call me that."

"-but my friends are already pretty fucked."

"It's all fun and games until someone loses an arm."

I was about to lay into him for that when Jade got between us. "My heart breaks for that poor boy," she said, placing a hand on my arm. "But maybe there's a silver lining in all this."

"Which is?"

She thought for a second. "I don't know yet. But it'll reveal itself. The Owl of Minerva spreads its wings at dusk."

Truth be told, I felt more like Wile E. Coyote than the Owl of Minerva. And I was once again doubting whether either of them had a clue, or whether they were just throwing ideas around confident that there would be no consequences – for them, at least. Abdul had already been maimed because Artemis was sloppy, and there was no guarantee he or Brady would ever be safe now that Nyhiloteph was onto them. Or Jackson. Not to mention everyone at Grad Oscars when Nyhiloteph's plan for the day - whatever it was - came to fruition.

Oh.

"Lucy? You okay?" Artemis snapped his fingers, bringing me back. I'd started to float in my inattention. I sank back to their level.

"I have an idea," I said, still feeling it around in my mind, "But it may be a bit over the top."

"Great," he replied, unenthused.

"Riddle me this." I began, "what is the only day we'll know for sure where Nyhiloteph will be at a particular time? When we can guarantee he'll be busy?"

"You're not thinking that Grad thing?" he asked.

"Why not? He barely talks about anything else, so we know he'll be there. And even if he senses something amiss, he won't be able to get out easily through the crowd."

The fortune teller raised an eyebrow. "There's method to her madness."

"We'll need to get your friends back on board," Artemis said. "Maybe find a vessel that isn't a Pringle can."

"Don't make fun of them!" I chided. "They didn't know what they were doing."

"I'm not laughing," Artemis said, the liar. His smirk was so wide it barely qualified as a smirk.

Jade blinked. "They tried to use a chip container to contain a demon?"

"Listen," I explained, "communication had broken down, they didn't really understand the vessel thing..."

Artemis doing a stoner voice: "Vessel? Is that like a boat, man?"

"Watch yourself," I snapped. "What would you suggest?"

Jade cut in: "Well, we know a wine bottle works."

"And you've got no shortage of those." That one came out with more snark than intended; Jade's face folded into the beginnings of a scowl. "It might be moot," I added hurriedly. "We need Abdul and Brady and we can only talk to them when they're a very specific type of high."

Jade laughed. "Dear, I've been contacting souls on the other side since before you were born. Doing it in reverse can't be too hard."

Chapter 36

I'd never done a "reverse séance" before, but I tried to convince myself Jade knew what she was doing. After all, she'd taught Artemis everything he knew. But that wasn't much.

It didn't help that she was hot and cold with me. Don't get me wrong – as a high school loser, I'd long internalized the adage "Not everybody's going to like you." But Jade's constant sniping was a real hindrance to our work. She'd initially been amenable to my plan to ambush Nyhiloteph, but after Artemis came around, she started finding fault with it. If I happened to agree with her on something, she'd reverse position. It was difficult to tell which of her objections were legitimate and which were pettiness - and my concerns, she discounted entirely.

"How do I know this won't kill him?" I asked, as we worked to get the seance room back to some semblance of its previous setup. "Or strand him in some sort of limbo?"

"My dear, the only 'limbo' will be when we dance at the victory party." Jade bent over backward to dip under the tabletop in the séance area, her spine cracking with a series of sickening snaps. I gave Artemis a look and he shrugged.

That was another problem. For whatever reason, Jade seemed to be permanently semi-sloshed.

"Can we take this seriously?" I asked. "I realize the term 'life or death situation' doesn't hold much meaning to us anymore, but I need my friends to make it out alive."

Jade straightened, spine clicking back into place, her lips as tight as a skull's jaw. Her voice dripped with condescension. "Of course - it would be absolutely terrible if someone died because someone else messed around with powers they didn't understand. Lucky no one here would do that."

Anger scorched my veins. "I wasn't the one selling ancient occult knowledge to any rando with a debit card."

"Lucy..." Artemis warned.

Jade snapped back. "Knowledge is neutral until applied, my girl."

"A book that summons a demon is neutral?"

"Its powers weren't invoked properly."

"The book was rigged!" I yelled. "It would have been impossible to get that ritual right."

"It was if your friends had cared to follow the instructions," she countered. "But maybe they didn't. Maybe they were improperly motivated."

Jade vanished in a burgundy plume, giving herself the last word. Which was wise, because I don't know what I would have done (could have done, if I'm being honest) if she'd stuck around.

I didn't need to read her mind to get what Jade was implying: she was saying my friends didn't really want me back. That they'd only attempted the summoning to alleviate their guilt. That there was a reason they'd half-assed it.

She stopped just short of saying I'd bewitched them.

What I did do was stalk down the stairs into the wine dungeon and start shattering things. I didn't even have to touch the shelves before red wine painted the walls, giving way to a rain of glass. When Artemis came down, the floor looked like an abstract canvass, and I was clutching the jagged neck of a bottle smashed to shards: Jackson Pollack meets Jack the Ripper. I dropped the broken pieces and picked up an intact bottle, aiming it at his head. "If you have anyone imprisoned in here, speak now."

"Please don't say that." The request was so quiet that I thought he was fading away again. But it was just his voice breaking. "She wasn't...imprisoned."

"I think she was," I argued. "That's why she's so bats-" I shut up about five seconds too late, just in time for Artemis's face to crumple. An alive person would have started crying, but Artemis started peeling, his ghost flesh giving way to the ripped, mangled, and now rotting skin of his body. It had never occurred to me to ask how Jade had wound up in the wine bottle.

"You trapped her?" I hissed.

He nodded. "It was after she died."

"No shit."

He continued in hasty whispers, his face knitting back into place. "I inherited the place but she was still here, haunting me... all she could do was throw things and scream sometimes. I tried to contact her, but I couldn't and she was scaring the shit out of me, driving away customers..."

"So you Secularly Exorcized her?"

"I thought she'd pass on - I thought that's what she wanted. I didn't realize she'd be stuck in the bottle for years fighting to get out."

I shuddered. "Does she know?"

"She hasn't said anything," he replied, voice upturned like a question.

"She's very hostile."

"That's just the booze, I think. And it's directed at you, not me."

"Yes!" I cried. "Because she knows she's pissed off and can't remember why!"

"Lower your voice, please."

I hadn't even felt it rising. "How dangerous do you think she'll be if she eventually remembers?"

"Are we gossiping down here?"

We both jumped as Jade appeared in the stairwell. I landed against another rack of wine that then collapsed, its contents crashing to the floor in a tsunami of glass and grape juice.

Had she been listening in? An image bubbled up in my mind: Jade's spirit exploding, flooding the room with merlot, dooming us to an eternity floating in a sea of it, like Artemis had done to her.

But she just chuckled at my mess and said, "Okay, you're cut off." The spilled wine floated up, red raindrops in reverse. Jade inhaled them, nostrils flaring and face turning ruddy. "Now, hurry on up kids, I can't clean this whole place myself."

It was like she had no memory of the fight. I waited until she was out of earshot and looked uneasily at Artemis. "Did she black out?" I mouthed.

He grimaced. "It wouldn't be the first time."

Presuming any of it could be evidence, the crime scene investigators had dumped Artemis's most obviously occult items in a cardboard box labelled "Black Magic misc" – which they promptly shoved in a corner and forgot about.

Even dormant and covered in dust, the crystal ball pulsed with a certain kind of life. Nestled between upside-down voodoo dolls and broken incense sticks, it still glowed faintly, its translucent fluid swirling with hints of purple and green. When Artemis reached in to pick it up, his fingers went right through it.

"Fuck."

"Is this a you problem, or..."

He scowled. "You try."

I gave it a shot. The crystal ball may as well have been empty mist. Or perhaps we were the mist.

"Maybe Jade can..." Artemis began.

"What, and smash it all over the floor?"

"I'd suggest taking a peek at my basement before accusing anyone else of breaking things," he retorted, slight emphasis on "my basement."

"That was intentional, in a rage," I replied. "I'm just saying, I wouldn't trust Jade with fine glassware."

"She hasn't broken any wine glasses yet," he reminded me. "That was one of her many skills – she always kept a steady hand, no matter how much she'd had to drink."

"A talented woman."

Artemis gave me a look.

I could tell it bothered him that Jade and I didn't get along. A warmer and fuzzier person would have tried to rectify that through forced bonding; I was grateful Artemis was not that kind of friend.

"She can give it a try," I conceded. "But I think this is just one of those objects ghosts can't lift. It's got too much power of its own."

He closed his eyes like a headache was coming on. That was one of his tics signalling a fervent wish to be anywhere else – usually when I was right and he was wrong.

I eyed the packing box. "We don't have to actually be sitting around a table to have a séance, right?"

"We need the ball as a conduit."

Kneeling by the box, I started tearing it open at the seams, bones and dolls and candles toppling with the cardboard sides. The Crystal Ball rolled, coming to a stop at the edge. "Can you do it from your knees?" I asked.

"Historically, yes."

I glared.

"There's no reason to think I couldn't conduct a séance from a kneeling position," he replied laboriously. "Other than, it'll be hard on my back."

"You're a ghost – how the fuck could you have back pain?"

"I had knee and back pain when I was alive. You brought all your problems with you into the afterlife, and I don't harp on you for that."

"Yes, you do!"

"Because you make your problems everyone else's."

There was a lot I could have said to that, but I didn't.

Chapter 37

When I left Artemis and Jade, they were sitting around the flattened cardboard box, crystal ball in the centre. Around them, the store was a war zone of gutted shelves and abandoned storage containers. The curtains had been removed, the officers' minds bedevilled by spectres hiding in their folds, and now slumped on the ground like a sleeping bog-beast. Flyaway pages, fallen from old books held together only by their shelf neighbours, littered the floor.

And dust, lots of dust. I didn't realize how much had accumulated until the cops came in and unsettled it.

It was a relief to be out on the porch, looking onto a robin's egg morning. It was dawn, the sky pale and the air cool; it felt more like autumn than late May, my favourite type of summer weather. I lingered, letting the promise of the day seep into me; for a moment I felt like I would be alive again when I stepped off the stoop, my future ahead of me, my options limitless.

A shadow fell over my mood when I thought of the dreams I'd never realize. I would never go to university, never get piss-drunk during frosh week, never have roommate drama other than bickering with Artemis. Instead of a first apartment, I had a store to haunt. Maybe one day I would relish my ability to fly, to read minds, to touch worlds beyond the veil - but at this stage in my death, it was the mundane I yearned for.

There was frost on the grass when I walked across the lawn. The blades didn't crackle under my feet.

I was more than a little wary about soliciting Abdul's help again. Especially not if it involved kidnapping and scaring the shit out of him. But Artemis didn't trust Brady to understand the instructions, and there was no one else.

The atmosphere over Abdul's lawn was thick enough to slice. The house, though it had the same grey bricks and white vinyl siding as the others on the block, looked duller, like I was viewing the place through a fog. I took a step into it and was driven backward by the oppressive miasma. Since the assault, Abdul had rallied to get back to school as soon as his doctor would let him. But that was the only area in which he was doing well. He came into class hot, participated actively, even aggressively, and then retreated into a cocoon even thicker than Jackson's had been. He ate lunch alone, ignoring even Brady when he tried to join him. He went straight home after school and buried himself in homework and video games.

Now I could keenly feel Abdul's grief and anger, the guilt and fear of his parents, the hurt feelings of his sisters, too young to understand why their brother had changed so fundamentally. When I tried again to cross the threshold, my arms prickled with goose pimples and I started to cough.

I told myself to suck it up. Artemis and Jade were doing the risky work; all I had to do was wait until Abdul's out-of-body-experience began and make sure to point his spirit in the right direction. ("And guard his body from invading forces," Artemis had added, like an afterthought). As I approached nearer to the house I started to breathe easier, even as the fog thickened; when I placed a foot on the first porch step I felt a faint electric charge, like shaking hands with a joy buzzer. A warning, but a weak one. I could hear voices muffled behind the door - Abdul's parents, speaking heatedly but quietly; I didn't need to eavesdrop to tell what about. Closing my eyes, I felt Abdul's presence above my head. Hiding in his bedroom. Same as Jackson, before I'd led him to Artemis.

"No," I said aloud, to no one in particular. "I'm not doing this again."

I could tell the séance had begun when the body started to twitch. We'd caught my friend in the middle of a nap, which made it easier, as a sleeping consciousness is already prone to drift.

I watched as his fingers spasmed and the tremors worked their way up his arms, elbows jerking, shoulders tensing and untensing, creating the illusion that he was shrugging repeatedly. What's going on? I dunno I dunno I dunno idunnoidunnoidunnow... His head was flung backwards, and I saw his Adam's apple sliding up and down his throat, like a light switch being flicked over and over. The symptoms should have been frightening to observe, I thought as his eyes rolled up to the whites, but they were so similar to what I'd experienced in my first and only séance, I wasn't too concerned. What I was worried about was noise; the house wasn't huge, and his mother was home. After the first round of bed-shaking seizures didn't summon her, I stopped fretting.

Brady's mouth fell open and coughed up a mist that caught in his throat before breaking out. His soul was a multicoloured shimmer, like oil on the surface of a puddle, and could have expanded to fill the room, perhaps the house. Instead, it gathered, forming a dense and vaguely humanoid mass that curled up like a fetus, softly glowing. A tendril of mist extended from the body and reached for me; I was tempted to touch it, to learn everything there was to know about Brady, and thus love him more than I already did. I believe there are very few people who you don't fall in love with once you experience the fullness of their being. But I resisted the temptation. Inhaling deeply, I blew on the spirit cluster, sending it towards Brady's open window. The bedroom faced east; from there he had a straight shot to the Grimoire.

"You two take it from here," I whispered to the mediums, though they obviously couldn't hear me. Artemis hadn't been happy with the change of plans, but once I refused to send Abdul, he'd had no choice but to agree. I just hoped Brady would rise to the occasion. Watching his spirit catch the current of the séance, pulled through the air above the rooftops like a flower dropped into a rushing stream, I believed he could.

Outside the room, the doorbell rang. I jumped, listening as footsteps crossed the hardwood. A click and hiss as the door opened, then a familiar voice chilled my non-existent bones. "Hi, Mrs. Thomas, is Brady there?"

It was Adrienne's voice, wielded with disarming sweetness by Nyhiloteph.

I prayed Brady's mother would notice something amiss. "I think he's sleeping," she said. I sighed. Then she added, "Feel free to knock, though!" and my heart sank again.

My mind whirled. Why was the demon here? Could he demon sense an unoccupied body nearby? I looked down at Brady, lying corpselike on top of his bedspread. His eyes were squeezed shut, like someone pretending to be asleep, and at some point his hands had lifted to clasp themselves on top of his chest.

Three gentle knocks. I held my breath, stupidly hoping Nyhiloteph would give up. When Brady didn't respond, the knob turned, door starting to open. Fortunately, I was an expert at slamming doors by this point. Nyhiloteph yelped, yanking Adrienne's fingers away just in time.

"Are you okay over there?" Brady's mother asked. She sounded farther away, like she'd gone back into the kitchen.

"Just goofing around!" Nyhiloteph called back. I snorted. He sounded like a boomer pretending to be a kid.

I pressed my body against the wood, readying for the next attempt at entry. I could slam a door, but could I hold one shut? And for how long? Then it hit me - it didn't matter. If Nyhiloteph did want to steal Brady's body, he could just vacate Adrienne's and drift through the walls. Adrienne would slump to the floor, Brady would sit up, and we'd be fucked.

I couldn't keep my eyes off him, defenceless on the bed, willing his spirit to return.

The doorknob twisted beneath me and the door flew open, sailing straight through me. Nyhiloteph stepped in.

I saw the demon in the girl's body examine my friend, confused at first, then perversely pleased. When his thoughtful frown started to curl, I made the decision.

Brady's body was an awkward fit. His torso felt loose, like I'd put on a sweatshirt two sizes too big (surprising in retrospect, because Brady was skinnier than I'd been). I was painfully aware of processes that had been automatic in life, breathing and blinking requiring effort. I could move Brady's legs, but not bend his knees, and even standing up from the bed required a weird combination of swinging his legs off the mattress and hopping up onto his feet. I reached for the headboard to steady myself, but Brady's fingers were like jelly; I couldn't even manipulate them, let alone grip anything.

Act natural, I urged myself, as I blurted out, "Good afternoon, Adrienne – what brings you here?"

Shit, that didn't sound like Brady at all.

"You okay?" Nyhiloteph asked.

Take two. "Yeah, man," I replied.

The demon cocked his head. "'Man?'"

I didn't know what to say. Nyhiloteph knew Brady was onto him, of course; was there any point in playing dumb? I decided Brady probably would – and besides, I didn't need to get into a drawn-out argument that would only expose me.

"I call everybody 'man,'" I said, trying to sound mildly stoned. "We're all mankind, right?"

Smirking, the demon replied, "You know that's not true."

Okay, Nyhiloteph was definitely onto me. But what could he do about it, us both in human form, Brady's mom in the next room?

I used the pregnant pause to try to figure out what to do next. Unfortunately, my mind-body coordination was not as sophisticated in this new body, so Brady's limbs acted on my first idea. I surprised even myself as I shoved my way past Nyhiloteph, stumbling into the foyer and falling facedown on the floor. A tsunami of copper flooded my mouth. Brady's mouth. Teeth jiggled in his gums.

Fuck, I'm a terrible friend.

Brady's mother ran into the room. I flopped in her arms like a rubber dummy. "Are you on something?" she shrieked, and Nyhiloteph rushed to my side, feigning concern.

"Oh my gosh, what's wrong with him?"

"I don't know – call 911!" Mrs. Thomas was cradling me, alternating between holding tight and trying to shake Brady senseless.

Nyhiloteph started dialling Adrienne's phone. "Ambulance," I heard him say, followed by the location. I thought it was very demon-like of him to know the street address without asking. "My friend's having some sort of seizure, I think he might be ODing or something…"

I was trying to free myself from Brady's mom's grip, arms flailing with no real will. She was holding me down, yelling "What did you take?!" over and over again. Disoriented, I closed my eyes to reduce the sensory overload; she thought I was losing consciousness and slapped me across both cheeks. I tasted more blood and felt a tickle in my throat; I realized what was happening just in time to stop myself from swallowing. I coughed; a pair of teeth flew from my lips and clattered across the floor like dice. Brady's mom screamed.

This went on for some time, until sirens cut through the din and Brady's mom dropped me. I winched as his head bounced off the floorboards. When I opened by eyes, Nyhiloteph was scowling at me and red and blue lights flashed up and down the windows.

Guess we're going for a ride.

The bilingual signage in the ER said the wait time would be about six hours. Brady's mother sat with me for about a sixth of that before wandering off to get herself a coffee. I couldn't blame her. It was an unpleasant place, each set of vinyl chairs walled by plexiglass as if to make you feel better about being surrounded by old people coughing. A redheaded kid with a fucked-up arm was sobbing inconsolably to my left (you don't know the half of it, kid), and to my right a woman with heart palpitations was engaged in passionate back-and-forth with an oblivious receptionist who had checked her in five minutes ago but now didn't recognize her and claimed not to have her on the list, only to realize out he'd been spelling her name wrong.

On the plus side, I had Brady's cell phone. I fired off a bevy of texts to Abdul, begging him to call me back, then scrolled through Brady's apps and chats. It felt like years since I'd used a smartphone, and it was a pleasant if mindless diversion. Pop rocks for the brain, my father used to call it. But I didn't want to think about him.

Brady's Instagram was full of sports memes and swimsuit models, the latter of which I liked, and I had to stop myself from declining Abdul's call when it came through.

"Brady, what the heck? You're in the hospital?"

"This isn't Brady," I said, in Brady's voice.

I heard the clatter as Abdul fumbled the phone, sighed as he scrambled to pick it up. It must have fallen somewhere out of reach, because it took a while. I could just barely hear him muttering as he struggled to get the phone in hand.

I don't know why being a ghost compels me to say spooky shit at the worst possible times.

"...Lucy?" Abdul ventured. He sounded out of breath.

"Yes."

"Where's Brady?"

"He's fine, he's with Artemis and Jade."

"Who's Jade?"

"The original owner of the creepy bookstore," I explained. "She's also dead. We had to bring Brady temporarily to the other side to talk to them, and I'm taking care of Brady's body in the meantime. Do you have a pen handy?"

"Yes, but - the other side?!"

"Brady will fill you in when he gets back, but I have limited time, so I want you to write this down." I hated putting Abdul through this flea circus again, and wished I had time to say something calming. But Brady's mother would be back any minute, clutching her paper cup of shitty drip. And there was another reason we were in a time crunch: when I looked up, the little glowing Brady fetus was hovering above me, waiting to be let in.

Chapter 38

Have you ever passed by a burning building and lingered behind the safety barriers, just basking in the chaos of firefighters running in and out and police directing traffic and looky-loos getting in the way? The panic and activity creating a palpable angry energy you can feel from down the street?

Yeah, I could tell a block from the Grimoire that Artemis and Jade were mad at me. When I got back to the store, I didn't even have a chance to wipe my feet and lock the door (neither strictly necessary, but things I liked to do to maintain some normalcy) before Artemis launched into me. "You possessed Brady's body?"

"How did you know?"

"Because he went back home and no one was there. It took us an hour to figure out where you'd went."

"Nyhiloteph showed up. I had to improvise."

"You don't improvise with the occult!" Artemis shouted. "What if you'd gotten stuck?"

"Well, I didn't"

Jade swooped down in a mist of wine. "I don't think you understand. The afterlife is off-limits to spirits whose bodies still live.

If you'd become trapped in that body, your friend would have been condemned to decades of conscious non-existence."

I bit the inside of my lip. "I was pretty sure I'd be able to get out."

"Pretty sure?!" Artemis yelled.

"Young lady, pretty sure is not enough when you're gambling with human souls."

And on and on and on like that.

Here's the dynamic: when Artemis reams me out for something, it's usually just his anxiety talking. It calms him to rattle off everything that could have gone wrong while emphasizing how I would be at fault if it did. I can deal with that. It was Jade continually cutting in that set my teeth on edge. The lectures. As if I hadn't risked my friends' safety countless times already. And as if I didn't already feel like shit for that.

Artemis again: "Shit, Lucy, it was bad enough you changing the contact person at the last minute–"

"You agreed to that," I reminded him.

"Because you refused to continue with the original plan."

"Because it wouldn't have worked! Like I said, I went to Abdul's house and I could tell he was in no state to retain anything. We would have broken his brain completely if we'd sucked his spirit from his body."

Jade cleared her throat, like she had something to say but wasn't going to until asked. When neither of us did, she stage-muttered, "I'm just saying, he seems to have been fine when you spoke to him on the phone."

"Because it was me, and we were just talking," I replied, straining to keep my tone even. "Doesn't mean he would have reacted well to an involuntary out-of-body experience. Abdul's already suffered enough, and I'm not going to subject him to further harm because Artemis was a square in high school and has an irrational hate-on for Brady."

Artemis scoffed. "Lucy, I don't know how to tell you this, but I don't give a shit one way or the other about your little friends."

"That's exceedingly clear," I shot back.

Jade raised her hands placatingly. "I think we should all calm down and discuss this in good faith."

"Will you shut the fuck up for a second?" I whirled around, jabbing an index finger at Artemis's face. "All of this is your fault, not mine, and has been since the very beginning. Botching seances, selling cursed books to teenagers – you refused to help me before this spiralled out of control and every single piece of advice you've given me since has been wrong. Do you even understand what you've been reading? Are you just skimming these big books? And then you have the nerve to shit-talk my friends for messing up rituals you yourself didn't know how to perform. Maybe if you weren't a fucking dilettante, none of this would have happened, and my friends would still be okay."

I regretted what I'd said even as I was saying it, but every word was another piece of kindling on my fire. Artemis sounded small, like a deflated balloon, when he finally replied: "You were the one who brought your friends to me."

"I've made mistakes since I died," I admitted. "I was emotional and I cared too much. You are either fucking stupid, or you're in league with the demon."

Jade got between us. "I think you should leave."

"In case you hadn't noticed, I'm haunting this place," I sneered. "So, what are you gonna do?" The question as directed at Jade, but I was looking into Artemis's eyes when I added, "Exorcise me? Because we know how well that works."

Artemis bit his tongue just in time, but his face was bright red. Jade narrowed her eyes, noticing the sudden quiet from both of us.

I told myself that there were multiple possible interpretations for my words: a jab at our earlier failed exorcism scheme, Artemis' general incompetence at occult matters. That Jade didn't have the context to discern what I'd really meant. But I didn't want to be in the room when she figured it out – and from the look on her face, I could tell that mine had given me away.

"I'll save you the trouble," I snapped, and shot for the door, fleeing confrontation on the pretense of storming out. I was halfway across the lawn when Artemis called after me. Shouting from the porch, wanting to follow but terrified to set foot outside the store. I wanted to apologize; instead, I quickened my pace.

Haunting my old house seemed like a no-brainer, so I drifted to the bungalow where my parents still lived. The place was a mausoleum.

The mantle was a shrine to me, my final school photo blown up to the size of an oil painting. The tables and shelves were crowded with framed pictures of me at various ages, and mementos I didn't even realize my parents kept: little clay snails and butterflies I made on ceramics day in grade three, construction paper Mother's Day cards, a garden rock I'd covered in glitter and inspirational quotes. Inexplicably on one of the end tables was a saltshaker filled with my baby teeth.

It was mildly tolerable until my parents got home from work, and then the mood went sour – worse even than it had been at Abdul's. Before I left, I unscrewed the cap from the saltshaker and arranged the tiny teeth into a heart shape on the coffee table – a message, I guess. Then I realized how disturbing and morbid that was and put them back.

I wandered aimlessly through the 'burbs for a while, looking into peoples' windows and imagining myself living their lives and understanding why Nyhiloteph wanted a human host. It was lonely out here, and my brief vacay into Brady's body hadn't lessened my yearnings. I could have stayed, I thought, frightened by how much the idea appealed to me. I was like an alcoholic, slipped a single shot of vodka after years of sobriety.

The sun was still up, somewhere, hidden under a thick cover of cloud. A shadow loomed behind me, stretching across the concrete at nightmare angles. A local homeowner out for an evening walk, I assumed, the late day's glare stretching his dark double to incredible heights. I ignored it for half a block, feeling safe in my invisibility. But the shadow stuck closely to my path, and I couldn't shake the being-watched feeling. When I turned the corner and still sensed it following behind, I concluded it wasn't human.

I stopped walking and my stalker halted in turn. I breathed deeply to quiet my nerves before turning around, prepared to do battle with Nyhiloteph, back on his home turf, or some as-yet-unknown demon from the canon. Instead, Artemis stood in the middle of the street, the shadow of someone's basketball hoop bisecting him.

I was so startled I almost didn't believe it. Artemis never left the store. Didn't believe he could leave the store. Paranoia seized me: what if this was some sort of trick, an as-yet unseen extension of Nyhiloteph's power to change forms? Alternately, Artemis had achieved significant personal growth and here I was, being weird about it.

I didn't approach. "Thought Jade turned you into a toad or something," I said, watching for his reaction. "Guess I kind of did you dirty, there."

The figure winced. "I hope you don't expect some emotional reconciliation, because I can't handle another one of those today."

I relaxed. That sounded more like Artemis. "So Jade knows, now?" I asked. "Did she take it okay?"

"Eventually," he said, waving the question off. He wouldn't want to rehash the conversation, so I didn't ask. I hung back for him, and we walked aimlessly together. The sky was starting to darken, the veiled sunset turning the clouds above a fiery shade of salmon.

"Was the talk with Brady okay?"

"Yes, actually. I maintain he's not going to go to school in Boston, but I think he retained the information this time. And Jade was really good with him. She's a bit more reassuring than I am."

"That's not a high bar to clear."

"That's why we got along so well when she was alive. She could tell me to calm down and I'd listen."

I couldn't help but notice he'd specified, "when she was alive."

"Jade and I started off on a bad note," I conceded. "But I guess, so did we."

"Don't think you don't still get on my nerves," Artemis corrected.

We passed under a telephone wire, and the crow who'd been perching on it took off squawking, like it was informing its brethren that we were on the move. When I looked up to watch it, I noticed other crows having their covert meetings on rooftops, croaking quietly. Conferring.

"I don't think any of us are our best selves in the afterlife," I mused.

He snorted. "I hate that concept. I never had a 'best self.'"

"That's what worries me sometimes," I admitted. "I think the good parts of us moved on already and it's just the dysfunctional, shitty parts of our spirits that got stuck here."

The idea was more self-pitying than anything, but when I turned around Artemis was looking at me funny. "I mean, you seem fine," I backtracked. "You're just here because we need your expertise."

Artemis burst out laughing.

Chapter 39

I wasn't psyched to face Jade again, even though she and Artemis were on better terms, so I let him head back ahead. I had one more apology to make.

Jackson had aged out of his *Firefly* fandom but still had the poster tacked to his wall. Knickknacks from his past life were arrayed, out of obligation rather than affection, along his bookshelves: a wood carving of an Atlantic fisherman, a memento of a family vacation; a miniature Lady Liberty from the school trip to New York; one of those plastic Furbies that were the hottest Happy Meal toy when we were kids; a stress ball shaped like a shark, its blue paint cracked from years of squeezing.

Jackson was ensconced in a swivel desk chair, bent over a jumble of worksheets and grid paper. I perched on top of his dresser, legs swinging over the edge. He looked over his shoulder only once, alerted by the rattling of the drawers, but wrote it off as the house settling and went back to his homework.

"I know you can't hear me," I said to the back of his head. "But I hope part of you can. I just wanted to say, I'm sorry I got you mixed up in this. It's all been my fault and you shouldn't blame yourself."

When had I last seen Jackson like this? Alone, himself, not under any spell? I checked myself: he was always under a spell. Nyhiloteph may have left him unattended, but wherever he went, he was on his master's leash.

I remembered the heft of the spell book in my hand, how perfect the weight of it was, how sure and straight it had flown from my hand to land, face-up, right in Jackson's line of sight. Like it was predestined. Why, out of all the books in the store, had I grabbed that one? What were the odds? But then, every game Nyhiloteph played was rigged, wasn't it? I pictured the book, behind my back, slithering forward, nudging itself past the book I would have picked up.

"We all got conned," I said, for my benefit as much as (who am I bullshitting? More than) his. "But somewhere in there, you know that demon isn't me. And I know deep down, you can hear me now. So, I'm going to try to get through to you."

He didn't stir.

"Remember how competitive we used to be? In every class we had together, your goal was just to beat my mark. We rarely had a conversation that didn't end up a sparring match. Have you and the demon even had an argument? Was that never a red flag?"

Really, I knew why Jackson'd been so deferential. It had nothing to do with me, and possibly not much to do with Nyhiloteph. It was Adrienne. When Jackson looked at Nyhiloteph he saw her face, maybe even sensed the crushed and mangled remnant of her spirit that hid inside. A girl he loved and yearned to impress. I'd never had a girlfriend, so I had no concept of how strong the hold could be. How our friendship that was so perfect and meaningful to me might be a stand-in for something stronger.

I always told myself I'd never be jealous of Jackson's future girlfriends. Because for all my possessiveness, I never liked him that way, could never, so when he found someone, I would never try to come between them. But maybe to free him from the demon's grip, that was what I had to do.

"I was the one who proofread your applications at one in the morning. I let your parents think I was failing math and needed your help so they'd unground you in time for Abdul's birthday party. Do you know how embarrassing that was for me?"

Did he care?

The intrusive thought was so alien, I almost mistook it for one of Nyhiloteph's subliminal messages. I shook my head to dispel it.

"The thing in Adrienne's body is nothing but selfish. His name is Nyhiloteph and all he does is take. He took everything from Adrienne and he's taking everything from you. Like, shit, he's coerced you into multiple felonies including aiding and abetting murder. Would I ever ask that of you?"

And would he have done it?

Of course, Jackson would, I told myself. He'd smeared filth on himself and stole a pig fetus to bring me back. Just, he'd neglected to notice I wasn't actually back.

No sound but the steady scratch of the pencil. Jackson was a lefty, like me, and the graphite smeared against the page and the side of his hand. Math homework, I surmised. Pen for everything else, but you must use a pencil for math. One of those hard-wired rules that was irrelevant to me now. Jackson preferred the refillable pencils, had once bought me a pack as part of a stationary-themed birthday present, even though I'd always been a No.2 girl.

"Was it that easy to forget me?" I asked. "Like, did you even know me at all?"

But had I been myself when I was with him? Or had I just re-shaped myself to fit into his life?

I was reminded of Adrienne's plastered smile as she begged her feuding parents to make nice, like it was her job to save them from embarrassing themselves. How desperate I'd been to save Jackson from himself, as if I could singlehandedly cure depression, as if my forgiveness meant so much it could bring him back from the dead.

People-pleasing. The most pathetic form of arrogance there is.

You'd force your friends to prove their loyalty, while deluding yourself that you were helping them.

My voice broke. "Did you actually want to bring me back, or did only you do it because you were bewitched?"

Jackson froze mid-equation, his spine suddenly rigid. Moving stiffly, as if he was afraid of moving too quickly and scaring something away, he spun to face the dresser.

And then the doorbell rang.

Of course, it was Nyhiloteph on the stoop. Pretty in pink, a spaghetti strap sundress and straw sandals, face shadowed under a floppy black sunhat. Jackson opened the door, but just enough to stick his head and shoulders out. He seemed...confused.

Nyhiloteph immediately started gossiping, something about Brady being on drugs. The same smear campaign he'd been working for weeks.

Jackson just blinked. "Brady's always been on drugs."

Nyhiloteph shook his head, his voice a respectful whisper designed to make Jackson lean closer. Jackson didn't.

"I went over to his place today to try to talk things out, and he was acting really weird." That was the demon's cue to invite himself into the house, where they could confidentially discuss such sensitive matters. He made a move for the door.

But Jackson stepped more firmly in the way of the entrance. The fibreglass door was half-closed, the storm door propped up by his palm, ready to slam shut as soon as he withdrew his hand. "It's not a good time, Adri - Lucy. I'm in the middle of something."

Nyhiloteph's jaw dropped. Jackson had never talked to him that way.

"Is something going on with you, Jack?"

"No? I'm just...studying."

The demon narrowed his cat-eyes. "Are you with someone?"

"No?" Jackson replied, not picking up on her implication. "Why would I be?"

"Oh. My. Gosh." The impression bordered on camp. Nyhiloteph wasn't even bothering to pretend to be me anymore. But the eighties valley girl accent wasn't right for Adrienne either.

"You might want to dial it back, Moon Unit," I said.

"I knew I heard someone!" Nyhiloteph shrieked. "I cannot believe you're going behind my back like this!"

Whatever Nyhiloteph's aim, it was backfiring – Jackson was more confused than anything. Even a brainwashed person can only believe so many contradictory things at once: he'd been dating Adrienne, before the possession, but he believed the girl in Adrienne's body was me, and he and I'd never dated, so why would I be jealous? And even if Adrienne and I had started to blur together for him, the accusation itself didn't make sense. As far as Jackson knew, no one else was in the room with him; there was no one for Adrienne to overhear. Nyhiloteph had overplayed his hand. One wrong move and the entire fantasy could shatter.

Nyhiloteph saw it too. His cheeks were turning red and his face looked tight, grinding his teeth as his mind worked overdrive. I watched expectantly, waiting to see what he'd do next, whether he'd right the house of cards or topple it.

Nyhiloteph started screaming. Nothing that made any sense in the context – just a stream of verbal abuse that gave way to gibberish; incoherent invective, like his mind had snapped. Which was the intent, I realized. Bravo, Hamlet.

Jackson flung open the door, rushed onto the stoop to comfort the hysteric. Nyhiloteph's shoulders were trembling, eyes blinking rapid-fire as his body collapsed on the porch. The caring boyfriend, Jackson knelt by his side, but recoiled without touching him. The body twitched. After a moment of hesitation, Jackson rushed inside to call an ambulance.

As soon as his back was turned, Nyhiloteph vanished.

Chapter 40

The door to the Grimoire was locked.

Sit with that for a minute. No door is locked for a ghost. But when I hurled myself against the wood, it was like I was corporeal again. I slammed, hard, the shock of the impact ricocheting though the memory of my nervous system. I swore, biting my tongue when I heard voices.

One voice, really, so loud it devoured the air, so loud I had no choice but to hear it. "You know, I've been very tolerant of your tomfoolery…"

Squinting through the frosted glass, I saw Jade and Artemis on their knees, Jade glowering defiantly, Artemis fetal and protecting his head. Standing before them was Nyhiloteph, lingering at some halfway point between his true form and his Adrienne impersonation.

He had Adrienne's body, her smooth skin and imperious face; but her blonde hair was a tangle and her toned arms and thighs were covered with thick fur. The fingers resembled human flesh, but were long and taloned. The feet – for the first time, not covered by his bulk – were featureless blocks. Nyhiloteph was a patchwork creature; not one part of him complemented any other.

The demon turned his head. "Ahh, Lucy," he said, as if I were in the room with them. The door swung open – inward, somehow, not the way it usually opened – sending me sprawling face-first onto Artemis's bloodstained floorboards.

I heard a second voice say, "More company?" and twisted my head to see the real Adrienne – blood-red lips, hot-pink eyeshadow to match the streak in her hair – leaning against one of the bookshelves. She was, one-by-one, plucking the most brittle volumes from their resting places and dangling them above a cigarette lighter, letting the flames lick at their edges until they caught. She should have been staring down Artemis as she did that, but her eyes were unfocused; she couldn't see him.

Nyhiloteph kicked me in the ribs. I let out a cry. I didn't realize pain could still hurt this much. "I am glad we could all be here together," Nyhiloteph continued. "Saves me time. I was saying, Lucy, that I've been very tolerant of you all – no skin off my nose, if you want to hang around here devising fanciful schemes – but you simply can't go around bringing back more and more people from the afterlife." He sneered at Jade. "Even if she is my biggest fan."

Jade went pale. "Excuse me?"

"I mean, you must be a fan," he said. "You bought my book. You drove six hours to that dead magician's estate auction for it; you were the only bidder. Then again, you didn't actually read it, did you? Just let it sit on a shelf looking impressive."

Adrienne tittered. "Just like my parents. Shelf after shelf of hardcovers, first editions, leather bound. Never opened, just on display to impress their elitist doctor friends."

"I should have burned that book," Jade snarled. She was on the floorboards, long legs crossed underneath her hips, like she'd been knocked down and hadn't untangled herself.

"And you should have had a husband who could have found you when you cracked your skull in the bathtub," Nyhiloteph retorted.

Artemis winced, and I couldn't block his signal before the image entered my head: Jade's naked body, stiff and waterlogged, crumpled at the bottom of a clawfoot tub; her foot was blocking the drain, and the three inches of sloshing water around was discoloured and murky. Artemis had been the one to find her, poor bastard.

"Some people can't plan ahead," Adrienne cracked, setting a book ablaze before stomping it out beneath her knee-high combat boot.

"You're not in this conversation," I shot back.

A foot drove into my chin, snapping my head to one side. The kick might have broken my neck, if I still had bones. "No sidebars," Nyhiloteph scolded. "I'm talking."

"Did you just come to shit-disturb?" I retorted, spoiling for a fight if only to clear Artemis's trauma from my mind. "I'm starting to think that's all you can do."

Nyhiloteph's eyes burned red. Averting my gaze from them, I noticed his legs ended with a set of two-toed black hoofs. Not quite goatlike, because goats have a certain charm. Nyhiloteph's feet looked severe, almost mechanical, sharp lines with a metallic sheen, like a brutalist sculpture of Pan. Each toe culminated in a sharp point.

One of those points was stained with something dark and sticky. I looked to my chest and found a red patch forming on my chest, below where Nyhiloteph had kicked me.

"You were saying?"

I reached to touch my throat, rubbing my hand along the bottom of my chin. It, too, came back bloodied.

Suddenly Nyhiloteph was in my face, the upraised fur on his neck and shoulders making him appear twice as large. "Don't ever think I couldn't put you down like a dog the second I get tired of playing fetch with you."

His breath smelled so rank, I couldn't control myself; I shoved him. He was so startled, it actually worked. He stumbled backwards, just a foot but enough for me to breathe again.

"I'm not afraid of you," I lied. "I know you can't live long outside Adrienne's body. You'll deflate like a balloon in a few minutes." Anticipating an escalation, I switched tactics, raising my voice to reach the living girl. "Did you hear that, Adrienne? He needs to eat you alive if he wants his freedom. Don't believe him when he says he'll let you live."

Adrienne cocked her head. I felt something click into place, like a pinball sinking into a trapdoor. Like my words had entered her mind and were being held somewhere, waiting to be let loose.

Nyhiloteph pounced. His freakish clawed fingers were so sharp, he could have slit my throat in one slash. I rolled out of the way, narrowly escaping. His offense botched, Nyhiloteph stumbled, landing chin-first on the floor. I tried to retreat, unwilling to take my eyes off him, but a bookshelf blocked my backward path. He was up in seconds, cornering me in three steps.

I assumed my friends would come to save me. If not Jade, then at least Artemis. But they were huddled behind Artemis's desk, rattling keys and fumbling with drawers. Thanks, guys.

Nyhiloteph grabbed me by the hair, wrenching my head backward. I yelped, and felt fingers lock around my jaw. Cold as steel bars. Grinning like a schoolboy, Nyhiloteph stuck out his tongue. It was long, black, and coated by a thousand sharp quills. He made sure I saw it, and went in for a kiss.

I recoiled as the tongue stretched toward my open mouth, but Nyhiloteph held me tight, pinning me against the bookshelf without releasing my jaw or my head. I tried to bite down, but my jaw was less powerful than his grip. The tongue was fully extended now, stretching six inches beyond his lips and hovering inches from mine, ready to force itself down my throat. The quills near the base were longer and thicker, perking up as if excited.

I was done for. He was going to shred my esophagus.

But the demon turned his head at a clatter from the desk. Adrienne jumped and stumbled, like she'd seen a ghost.

What Adrienne would have seen was a rippling sheet of paper, hovering in midair. It was Jade who brandished it, standing on Artemis's chair to add authority to her five-foot frame. I expected some crumbling rune or ancient scroll, but upon inspection it was a standard eight-and-a-half-by-eleven, dog-eared and creased, yellowed only because it was yellow printer paper. The Government of Ontario logo was stamped on one corner.

"Demon!" she howled, her voice echoing through the shop almost as loudly as Nyhiloteph's could. "As the lawful owner of this domicile, I command you to vacate!"

My head snapped forward as Nyhiloteph let me go, stepping away and reverting back into Adrienne's human form. No fur, no hooves – just a teen girl scowl.

"You don't own this building anymore," he argued, his voice flat and brittle, like a crow's. "Your protection spell has no force or effect."

She rustled the papers, still held high. "I have a deed with my name on it."

Nyhiloteph hesitated, looking at me and then back at her. Artemis, for his part, was cowering behind the desk, crouching so only the top of his head was visible.

The real Adrienne had stuck a finger into one ear, as if an episode of tinnitus had just come on; some of the conversation, or at least its reverberations, was getting through to her. "Nyhil, what's going on?"

"Real estate dispute," the demon growled.

"The ownership of the property may have been transferred after my death," Jade continued, "but the protection spell did not. I still have the final say over which entities are allowed to cross over this threshold."

"Horseshit!"

Jade nodded in my direction. "If you want to test my interpretation, go ahead. But if you're wrong, you'll be sent back to the plane you came from. You're still bound by the rules, as well as any of us."

I could see him considering that, eyeing me hungrily. Regretting terrorizing me when he could have just killed me. He snapped his head toward Jade, the glare from his red eyes lighting up the document as he read it, searching for some kind of loophole, some sign of fraud or fakery. I saw his fists clench.

"If you think I'm wrong," Jade said again, gesturing towards me. "Have at her."

I thought he was going to chop my head off as part of his dramatic exit. Instead, he inhaled, taking a long whiff of my hair, and turned up his nose in insult. "I'll play with my food a while longer," he announced, spitting.

Adrienne's quizzical expression broke into a disjointed rictus as the demon forced his bulk through her mouth, disappearing inside her. Adrienne burped and the look in her eyes changed, Nyhiloteph once again behind the controls. I tried not to tremble as he headed for the door. Hoping it wasn't a trick, hoping Jade wasn't bullshitting, hoping my fear wasn't loud enough to reach him.

"Oh, Madame?" Nyhiloteph said, not turning around. Adrienne's voice, now.

Jade cocked her head.

"You can have your shack here, at least until they send the bulldozers in, but everything outside it is mine. I'd think carefully before crossing the threshold."

The spit gob Nyhiloteph had hocked was smoking, burning a little hole in the floorboards. It stung my heel when I stomped it out.

Chapter 41

That Monday, Abdul and Brady reconvened at lunchtime. It was their first chance to talk since the incident; Brady's mother had grounded him over the weekend for reasons even she couldn't articulate.

"Do you ever think we might be losing our minds?" Brady asked, chugging a Monster energy drink.

"I think the physical evidence is undeniable," Abdul retorted. His attention was fixed on the plate of food in front of him, leftover baasto that he was struggling to eat one-handed. Noodles that he would have ordinarily twirled on a spoon were slipping off his plastic fork, sending spiced meat sauce spattering across the tabletop.

Brady ran his tongue across the new gap between his teeth. "Yeah, I got the worst of it for sure."

"You look like a hockey goalie."

"I heard chicks dig hockey players."

Abdul rolled his eyes. "Did you know the guidance counsellor sent me a bunch of amputee scholarships to apply to?"

"Seriously?"

He nodded. "While I was still in the hospital."

"Did you apply?"

"I submitted something, but I don't know how coherent it was." He was holding his fork sideways, slicing the squirming pasta into bite-sized chunks that he tried to coax onto the tines. "I'm afraid to look at the essay again, I probably sounded like a lunatic."

"Yeah, my mom wants me to see a shrink. I heard her on the phone with my aunt saying she caught me rambling about demons." That earned Brady a funny look from a sophomore walking past with a cafeteria tray. He raised his voice to add: "Which totally aren't real."

"Nice catch."

A musical laugh rang out from across the plaza, seeming to ride across the breeze. The boys turned to look. "Speaking of," Abdul said.

At the other end of the lunch yard, Adrienne was sitting on top of one of the picnic tables, holding court to a group of band geeks, chess champions, punk rockers, athletes, loners, popular kids, and smoking pit stoners who were hanging on her every word.

Part V:

Read 'Em and Weep

Chapter 42

Grad Oscars Day at Tom Thompson High. The glitz, the glamour – not really. More like streamers and cardboard stars tacked to the walls.

Oh, and a star of salt encircling the building, but the Committee had no part in that.

Weak from fasting, Brady's arm shook has he hauled the bag of road salt from the edge of the front yard, along the left side of the school, and out into the athletic field. Supervised by Abdul - who'd worked out the angles - he poured deliberately, wary of waste, but making sure there were no gaps. He was being careful, Abdul had to admit, but he couldn't help but wonder if Brady had been as conscientious in private. If he'd really abstained from food and smoking and caffeine for three days like Jade had instructed. If he'd spent as many hours practicing the incantation as Abdul had, perfecting his pronunciation of the Latin script.

I wondered that, too, but I wasn't in any position to do anything but hope. And maybe I wasn't too deluded in hoping for the best. After all, we'd started out in an impossible situation: me unable to communicate, my friends blissfully ignorant of the threat in their midst. When I thought of how alone and helpless I'd been in the early days of my death, it was almost unbelievable how far I'd come.

Don't second guess a miracle.

Shanna winced as the nominee pin pricked her. "Ow!"

"Oops," Nyhiloteph said, blue eyes glinting.

Shanna rubbed her wound as the line moved along, inspecting the pin on her breast. It was cut from orange felt, shaped vaguely like a pom pom, and read, "Most Spirited." I could hear her thoughts as she wondered what that even meant, assuming it to be a pity nom: Adrienne wanting to do something nice for the nerd who whined about being excluded. How else could she explain ending up in the same category with Alanna from Drama Club?

I also wasn't sure what Nyhiloteph's game was there. But while Shanna felt patronized, I knew to be worried. The second I laid eyes on him, my wounds – the ones he'd given me – started to weep.

Behind her, George hissed as he was jabbed. His pin was brown felt and shaped like a football. He'd been nominated for Best Sport.

As I watched the parade of contenders, I started to notice commonalities – namely, at least a third of them didn't make any sense. The Committee's original rigging had had a flattening effect, limiting most of the awards to their friends. Nyhiloteph had done the opposite, putting nerds and introverts and alt kids up alongside the popular crew. Some of his picks felt like jokes - for fuck's sake, Destiny was in the running for Most Congenial – but many were passive-aggressive. Hence, you had Justin the punk drummer competing against Bassoon Pat and Mr. Jones' lead trumpeter for Best Musician. Jackson and Adrienne, of course, were nominated for Best Couple. When it was time for him to get his pin, Nyhiloteph jabbed him hard enough to draw blood.

At the next yelp of pain, Kerri leaned in. "I think people can put those on themselves."

"And where would be the ceremony in that?" Nyhiloteph asked. In a few weeks of teenage girlhood he'd perfected this wide-eyed innocent look with an edge of don't-fuck-with-me. No one ever challenged him.

Kerri averted her eyes.

The nominee list was sweaty and dogeared from Nalo's fidgeting. The microphone screeched as she leaned in. "And the Nominees for Most Likely to Succeed are…"

"Us," I said.

Jade and I had squeezed ourselves behind one of the cafeteria tables that had been folded up against the wall for the awards ceremony. Against her chest, Jade protectively cradled the wine bottle that was to be the demon's vessel.

"Don't jinx this," she warned.

"I never took you for superstitious."

She narrowed her eyes at me – not quite a scowl, but not not a scowl. Jade and I had made our apologies, and I had to admit she'd been a godsend for our mission, but neither of us would say we liked each other.

"Isn't it important to believe in yourself if you want a spell to work?" I asked.

"Actually, it's the opposite," Jade said. "It's the failure of humility before the great powers that causes things to go haywire."

"Well fuck, then. Makes me wish Artemis were here," I replied. "He'd keep us from getting too optimistic."

"I'm glad he's not."

Because you don't want him to get hurt, or because you think he'd self-destruct?

"Both," Jade replied to my unsaid thought. "Love the boy, but he was always–" She fell silent with a shudder. "Did you feel that?"

I nodded. A cold, jarring sensation, like a cell door slamming shut.

"The star is formed."

That meant the boys would start the exorcism momentarily. Nyhiloteph would be expelled from Adrienne's body, and Jade would swoop in with the wine bottle just as they were reciting the binding spell. It was precarious but precisely timed. We'd rehearsed earlier in the week, Jade flying from one end of the empty caf to the other while Abdul timed with a stopwatch, Brady beside him mouthing the incantation; the janitor who walked in hadn't quite believed their explanation that they were practicing a speech.

I saw Nyhiloteph stiffen for a moment as he grabbed the mic, feeling the same thing we did. He shrunk as if bracing for something, and his head turned to scan the room. I tensed up, waiting. But nothing happened. Nyhiloteph relaxed and started to speak.

"Before we announce the winners, I wanted to say a few words. I know this year has been...particularly difficult for many. A lot of us have suffered losses, a lot of us are grieving, including some people very close to me."

"Of course, it's all about her," I heard someone mutter.

"In light of the tragedies, the Committee and I decided to create a special award."

"That's the dumb tribute they're doing for me," I said to Jade. "Wonder what they have in mind."

Nyhiloteph looked at Kerri, who was fumbling with the projector. "We ready?"

"Ready when you are."

Nyhiloteph smiled. "There were so many exceptional people we wanted to recognize with this award, we figured it would be easier to show them onscreen. Without further ado..."

The projector flickered to life, and the screen on stage lit up. The image was a basic PowerPoint slide, a long, bulleted list in a sans serif font. The category title was "Best Revenge."

The entire student body inhaled sharply, at the exact same moment.

Every wrong that Nyhiloteph had caused was listed, next to victim and perpetrator: "Justin Seamus – Tuba Sloppy Joe (Mr. Jones)." Etcetera. He'd even given a whimsical name for each.

Destiny's tripping incident had been titled, "Trouble Afoot." The lab accident was "Burn Baby Burn." There were a dozen nominees, incidents I hadn't witnessed and could only guess at.

There was a moment of shock, of stillness - and then a wave.

Alanna whirled around, nostrils flaring (nose newly heeled, now with a slight rightward bent) as she snarled like an animal. "You fucking bitch, I knew you did that on purpose!" She lunged at Shanna, knocking the chess-master to the ground, and raked her fingernails across Shanna's face. "See how you like being disfigured!"

George rushed to help his co-chair, only to be tackled by the rest of the Best Sport crew.

"Not so fast, nerd."

"What, think you're better than us?"

Scars shining, Alanna opened her mouth and dug into Shanna's throat, coming up with a strip of flesh. Her new fake front teeth, slightly whiter than her old ones, glinted under the fluorescents.

Whatever was happening, it wasn't simply a catfight.

Mr. Jones had been staring daggers at Justin from the crowd, and now rose from his chair. "It was you, wasn't it! I knew it was an envious punk like you who sabotaged my band!" His hands were white-knuckled with rage, gripping the back of the seat in front of him.

"Man, I don't know what you're -"

Justin's jaw dropped when Jones picked up the chair and hurled it at him. He dodged the projectile but stepped too far and tumbled off the stage, cracking his head on the floor. Jones jumped onto his back before Justin could regain his senses, yanking his head up by the hair to direct a flurry of punches at his face.

"You people hate beauty! You *filthy degenerate punks* are enemies of all that is *decent* and *meaningful* in this world!" Each word of filthy degenerate punks was accentuated with another blow. He grabbed Justin's throat at enemies and decent and meaningful marked the start of the strangulation. Blood bubbled from Justin's lips.

Similar scenes erupted all along the stage. The quirkiest Best Dressed nominee was stripped and stomped on, her competitors draping themselves in her clothes as they took turns kicking her in the ribs. Two of the Best Couples were going at each other in a bloody tag team match. Destiny's figure was all-but buried under a pile of popular girls, ripping her dress and pulling at her hair.

"Knock her teeth out, ladies!"

Jade grabbed me and we floated above the crazed throng. Below us, it looked like at least a third of the crowd was involved in some sort of fight, with only a handful of teachers trying to break things up. The unaffected students rushed the doors, practically climbing over each other to get out faster. Several lay trampled on the ground. I was trying to block it all out when I heard a familiar cry amid the clamour.

A cornered Jackson was brandishing a chair, descended upon by Paul Sharma and two guys from the hockey team. I didn't get the significance at first, then remembered they'd all gone out with Adrienne sometime between seventh grade and now – so in their demon-addled brains, Jackson had stolen their girl. Thinking quickly or not at all, I broke rank and glided toward him. The chair flew from Jackson's hands and through my chest to bounce off Paul's knees. "That all you got?" the honour roller sneered, continuing his advance.

Something clicked. "Shit!" Jackson yelled, and backed into the wall, eyes wide. I followed his gaze. One of the hockey players had a Swiss Army Knife, and it wasn't the nail file he'd opened. Summoning my full reserve of physicality, I knocked it out of his hand. Several of the guys pounced for it; I didn't see who won.

"Lucy! A little help!" Jade was almost at the stage, wine bottle floating with her. Nyhiloteph's head turned the same time as mine did. Adrienne's body collapsed as the demon left it.

No one ran to help her as her body collapsed, wracked in agony. Her jaw was opening like a snake's to belch a deluge of thick black gunk, the same that I'd seen spurt out of Mr. Anderson, but in a much larger quantity. The ooze shaped itself as it emerged, lengthening into a nude, grey-skinned simulacra of its host, which launched itself off the stage and toward Jade. It happened too fast for either of us to do anything. The bottle fell from Jade's hand as taloned fingers plunged into her gut.

I'd never asked Artemis if a ghost could be killed. As Madame Jade went pale and her face fell to blankness, I knew we could.

Nyhiloteph was wrist-deep in her abdomen when he saw me watching. Grinning with blackened teeth, he jerked his arm up, ripping a vertical wound for dramatic effect. A torrent of crimson liquid flowed from the hole, streamed to the floor, and disappeared. Its scent lingered in the air. Red wine. When I looked up from where the puddle should have been, Jade was gone.

The demon whirled around, hissing as he saw me. "I should have known it was you. Here to ruin my special day."

I didn't know what to do. I didn't even know what had happened. Abdul and Brady should have finished the incantation five minutes ago. This should be nearly over. Now Nyhiloteph was free, of his own accord, Jade disappeared, the vessel likely smashed. What the fuck, guys?

"When my kids went to school here, they had a butterfly garden."

Outside, Abdul and Brady nodded along as Esther McGarry reminisced. Esther lived near the school, had sent her sons there when they were teens, thirty years ago, and still strolled along the grounds on sunny days. She'd been widowed three years ago, was lonely, and liked to talk to young people. She was harmless and the students who encountered her were told to be nice.

Today, my friends could have afforded to be a little meaner.

"Raised the monarchs from the caterpillar stage. They started right in September, then in the fall they'd fly off to Mexico. The teacher threw a little party for them, I remember. Carl had his photo in the community news…"

Abdul looked at Brady helplessly. Neither of them had an idea. Abdul had told her the salt lines were the beginning of a rock garden, and it had only encouraged her.

"Oh well, I suppose times change. What did you say you were doing again?"

I snapped back to reality. Nyhiloteph had sent me this vision, wanted me to know that help was not on the way as he sailed towards me, pink-painted nails sharpened and gleaming.

Below my feet, Adrienne body wheezed- she was still inside but not fully inhabiting it. Her spirit seemed so weak that anyone could have overpowered it. That gave me an idea: I couldn't fight Nyhiloteph, but I didn't have to.

I waited until he was seconds away from slicing me open, then ducked and dove for Adrienne's body. He'd made a mistake leaving her unprotected. I thought myself small, compressing myself until I would fit into Adrienne's mouth. Flew toward her lips. I bounced back, landing on my ass.

Adrienne sat up, laughing. I thought Nyhiloteph had beaten me to her, but when I looked up, he was still trailing me.

"Adrienne?" I gasped. "Can you see me now?"

"Right through you," she replied. "You've really become everything you used to fight against, haven't you?"

"I would have given your body back," I said. "I don't think he will."

Adrienne sat cross-legged, grinning up at me like a defiant child, her teeth still stained with the monster's afterbirth. I could feel Nyhiloteph inching closer. "Nyhiloteph's given me so much more than a body."

"Nyhiloteph stole your life," I argued. "He sabotaged all your friendships, he killed your parents, he–"

"Freed me," she said coldly. "Nyhiloteph taught me to be myself - to do what I want, take what I want, live without shame. Without guilt."

"Adrienne," I pleaded, even as I sensed the demon looming behind me. "He's going to kill you when this is all over. That's why he's learning to copy you – he's going to destroy your body and steal your identity."

She frowned at me pityingly, rising to her feet. "No, silly. He's helping me be in two places at once."

"So you can be his alibi," I retorted. "What exactly do you think is going to happen here, Adrienne? Is the plan really to let him parade around looking like you, while you, what, live your normal boring suburban life? I could see if you were getting an alternate body, too, but what are you even getting out of this?"

"You don't understand." Her blue eyes were twin glaciers. "All my life, I tried to be perfect. Perfect grades, perfect attendance, perfectly kind to all creatures, even though I knew I was superior to all of them." She snapped her fingers. "But all that can go away in a second. Like when you kill some dork by accident and suddenly the cops are taking your bloodwork and your friends don't want to be in photos with you anymore and everyone stares at you when they think you can't see and then averts their eyes when you look their way, like you're a freaking murderer."

"You're not," I told her.

She grinned. "But I am, and it's fantastic."

A shadow overtook me, and Nyhiloteph grabbed me from behind, wrenching my arms behind my back, his prickles digging into my skin. A tingling pressure against my crotch as the demon's erection pressed against me, poking up from between my legs like a hook to hold me in place. I tried to wriggle away, but the prick expanded, rising to meet my eyes – and it wasn't a penis but a fucking snake, a green-and-black boa that sprouted from his crotch and opened its mouth to reveal rows of needles. I screamed. The snake seemed to cackle, jaws spreading wider. I believe it would have taken a chunk out of me right then, had Adrienne not been enjoying my reaction too much.

"I just watched the first murder – your friend there. That's my biggest regret. I wish I'd gotten a chance to help re-arrange that rude freak's face."

I flushed, indignant for poor Artemis. "You must have had fun killing your parents."

She responded with a little eye-roll and a bless-your-heart kind of smile. "That wasn't my idea either, but I was definitely on board after the fact. They stifled me."

The snake curled around me, wrapping me tight from ankles to shoulders. There was no way I could break the hold; the only thing I could do was keep Adrienne talking, stall for time and hope some other solution would come to me.

"All your friends," I countered, "all these other people you barely knew – what did they ever do to you?"

She was looking increasingly exasperated, like a teacher with a student struggling to grasp a basic concept. "That was the problem, Ghost-Girl. They didn't know me. They only cared about the small part I allowed them to see – the nice, pretty, popular girl who always made the best posters." Her tone was becoming more and more hysterical, and her eyes welled with tears. "They never even thought there might be more to me."

"How narcissistic are you?!" I yelled. Behind me, I felt Nyhiloteph shaking – laughing at me. Unable to gesture with my hands, I jabbed my chin at the carnage around us. "Congratulations, everybody finally knows the depths of your depravity. Is that what you were hiding all these years? Is that what you wish your friends had seen in you?"

I might have had a better chance of escape by appealing to Adrienne's better angels – but they'd left her shoulder long ago. The snake gave me a squeeze, a reminder that it could crush my lungs in an instant.

Adrienne shook her head. "That's the irony – they don't. When everyone's dead, I'm going to walk out of here a survivor. A perfect victim." She looked over her shoulder, watching a phys. ed. teacher gnawing at an unconscious sprinter's Achilles tendon. "I'll never truly get over what happened here."

I could grasp the plan. Adrienne living out her days on her parents' money while Nyhiloteph fed off her energy. Daily fainting spells as their fused spirits vacated her body, which would remain under medical supervision while they ran wild. Witnesses might see a killer matching Adrienne's description, but no one would seriously suspect the catatonic trauma patient.

"His powers, your looks and charm," I said wryly.

"Friends forever," she replied. "We'll eat, drink and make merry while the old me sleeps. Perfect as I always was."

"Living out your worst fear," I continued, the snake's head burrowing into my hair. I felt its mouth open, teeth against my head like it was measuring whether it would fit. "All this bullshit about being perfect, how no one ever saw the real you – you've made your life small for other people. Now you're making it even smaller for him."

Her smile faltered.

"How did Nyhiloteph liberate you, really?" I pushed. "A makeover and some cannibalism. You didn't need demonic possession for that. You could have gotten a nose ring any time."

Unfortunately, punk Justin picked that moment to stumble into our path. His face and ears were dotted with jagged holes where Mr. Jones had ripped out each of his piercings; his hair, dyed pylon-orange, flapped like a toupee, scalped flesh barely hanging on. The laces in his combat boots were undone, and he tripped without trying to catch himself, skidding across the floor chin-first. Adrienne flipped him over so his shellshocked eyes gazed at the ceiling, and stepped on his throat with a smirk. The pressure was enough to pop a hole in the shellshocked punk's neck, her kitten heel piercing his voice box. He let out a squeak, legs and arms spasming and flailing, but didn't otherwise fight back. His mind was already gone; I hoped, mentally at least, he was in whatever heaven his empty eyes were fixed on.

Adrienne plucked out the last remaining ring, tearing a hole in his nostril, and jabbed the post into her own septum, her tongue flicking up lick the trickle of blood. "Like this?" she asked mockingly. "Or should I try something more drastic? Maybe dye my hair?" Nyhiloteph giggled as Adrienne bent over to grab the loose edge of Justin's scalp, like turning over a rock. I shut my eyes; when I opened them, Justin's dishevelled orange mop was sitting jauntily atop Adrienne's hair, his blood dripping down her scalp.

"Your superficial teenage rebellion is fleeting. Mine is eternal."

It was Adrienne's lips that moved, her voice that spoke. But in Nyhiloteph's grip, I could feel the rumble coming from his throat. He was putting words in her mouth.

Justin's scalp was slipping like a bad toupee. It left a red smear across her cheek when it sloughed off her head, landing on the cafeteria floor with a sickening squelch.

"Fucking poser," I sneered, and suddenly Nyhiloteph lifted me off my feet. I shrieked. The snake tightened its hold, its pressure concentrated at my ribs. This time, it didn't let up; I opened my mouth but no air reached my lungs. A few minutes in this position and I'd be smothered.

"I'm tired of these culture wars," he declared. "Adrienne, do you have anything you want to add before I swallow her?"

"Do me a favour?" she asked.

"Anything."

"Eat her one bite at a time."

The stakes were finally setting in. I was about to die – again. I didn't know what that looked like, except it wouldn't be merciful. "He's lying to you. Adrienne!" I cried. "He's going to take everything from you and abandon you!"

Adrienne laughed, "So desperate. Like you al-"

She stopped mid-sentence, twitching.

"Always what?" I asked, as her head snapped back. Her eyes, bulging out of her head, changed colour for a second, irises swirling with milk. She shook her head, and when she looked at me again the blue had returned. But it was undeniable what was happening.

Esther McGarry had left. Abdul and Brady had started the exorcism, demanding the spirit vacate Adrienne's body. But Nyhiloteph was no longer inside the body, and it was Adrienne who was being expelled.

Nyhiloteph dropped me as another wave knocked Adrienne off her feet, snake unfurling with a hiss. He rushed to her side like a combat nurse. But instead of tending to her, the demon roared into her ear, like he was trying to startle her out of the spell's influence. The soundwaves rattled the foundations, sending a ceiling tile crashing to the ground. But it wasn't enough to drown out the exorcism rite, which came to us on a wavelength that had nothing to do with the physics of sound. The gently repeating words even churned in my ears, like hearing the echo of the sea in a conch shell.

Adrienne crossed her arms and drew her legs together, massaging her flesh with her hands to maintain a hold over her body. Her face was contorting into exaggerated, semi-impossible shapes, like a clay model being re-shaped. The re-arrangement was radical enough to smear her make-up, mascara speckling her cheeks and lipstick smears on her forehead.

Nyhiloteph loomed over her like a weightlifting coach, barking commands. "You're stronger than they are! Don't let them take what's ours!"

Adrienne slapped herself, and when that didn't work she closed her fist and punched herself in the chest. "That's good," Nyhiloteph growled. "Ground yourself in pain." He was obviously getting off on her hurting herself, of course – but it also seemed to be working. Her face, red with exertion, was no longer twisting like dough, and her muscle spasms were easing.

Adrienne wasn't going to leave her body without a fight, so I decided to give her a little push.

Chapter 43

I'd been a poor fit for Brady, but sliding into Adrienne's body was another sensation entirely. Like inserting a finger into yourself, wincing but not retreating as your body protests, folds of skin and then hard walls parting until you're no longer an invader but a welcome guest. Slipping into Adrienne's arms, legs, feeling my breath fill her lungs and expand her chest, running my tongue against her teeth – it was like sinking into the arms of a lover.

I came to staring out of Adrienne's eyes – directly into an identical set. Adrienne's ghost hovered over me, face flushed with rage, her demonic BFF by her side.

Shaking with unfamiliar limbs, I climbed to my new knees and fell forward, conking my head on the floor. "Fuck." I looked up to see the spirits circling. They were taking their time, confident that I could never escape them even if I managed to get away. Vultures who knew I was already dead.

I pushed myself into a standing position, only to feel Nyhiloteph's claw slap me across the face. My head snapped so hard I thought my neck would break. Adrienne's neck. As the force of the blow knocked me down, I mulled letting him do just that. Fighting back half-assedly until Nyhiloteph eventually killed me. With Adrienne's body uninhabitable, they'd have nowhere to go, and hopefully Nyhiloteph would have exhausted his earthly powers.

Nyhiloteph was larger than he'd ever been, swollen like a tick with the bloodshed he'd inspired. He inhaled, and his out-breath flattened me. It was rank, and came out of him with enough force to pin me to the floor. It was like standing in a wind tunnel made of human flesh.

Okay, fuck my earlier plan. I did not want to live through whatever foul death he had in mind for me. Fearful of sitting up and bringing myself closer to him, I slithered away on my back, moving at a snail's pace, hands scrabbling across the floor as if reaching for a weapon, something, anything that could...

The wine bottle.

It was here, and it was intact. My hand wrapped around its neck, feeling the cold glass against my palm. If only, I thought. That's when I remembered I was human now, with all the privileges and powers of humanity. I didn't need Abdul or Brady to say the magic words.

Propped up on my elbows, I lifted the bottle and pointed it towards Nyhiloteph, mouth-first. My hand trembled, but my voice didn't as I recited the binding spell.

I slipped on a pool of blood as I ran across the caf, skidded until I almost tripped over its source. Class Clown Carter Daniels, strangled by a microphone cord, jaw forced open so the mic head could be shoved down his throat.

I held the wine bottle closer to my chest, terrified of dropping it. The glass glowed with a swirling, angry light. I couldn't see Adrienne's spirit, now that I was human, but I had no doubt she was chasing after me. To reclaim her body, or rescue her bestie, I had no idea. There were more pressing horrors to flee.

Nyhiloteph's defeat hadn't put an end to the carnage. The cafeteria was now filled with the sounds of smacking and tearing and slurping as the blood-crazed victors ate and drank. Anyone who'd sought escape had already burst through the doors – the ones who'd made it out, that is. One girl, not quite dead, screamed as the student council president flayed her with a nail file. The VPs of Academics, Athletics, and Social Affairs held her down.

I took one last look at the projection screen. At some point during the brawl, someone had clicked to the next slide.

Special Memorial Award:

Lucy Steinberg - Best Friend

One final insult.

The hallways were empty when I fled through the side door, the school under lockdown. A few feet from the caf doors, to the right of a display case, Jackson sat with his head in his knees. He jumped when he saw me.

"Get away!" he yelled, his voice quavering.

Tightening my grip around the bottle, I raised my other hand. "Jackson, it's Lucy."

I looked to his shaking hand and saw he was holding the Swiss Army Knife. I guess he won that fight after all. His arm was extended, just a slight bend in the elbow, pointing the blade at my chest. I remembered again how human I was.

"Please put that down and just listen to me for a second." He didn't lower his arm, and I rattled off the story before he could do anything rash. "Adrienne was possessed by a demon, and he was pretending to be me." Jackson shook his head, face scrunching. "He's gone now. I had to go into her body to get her out."

"Shut up." My friend was crying, muttering to himself, the events of the last few minutes – months, really – finally too much for his sanity.

"Ask Abdul and Brady," I begged. "They did the exorcism, they're outside right now."

He choked on a sob. "I don't believe you. I don't even know who you are."

"Jackson, please, I'm Lucy! I'm really-"

The knife plunged into my sternum.

Chapter 44

Jackson didn't let go, just gripped the handle and stared. I felt the soles of my feet flat on the ground, the knife that stretched from my heart to Jackson's hand the only thing holding me upright. He opened his fist and I fell. Pain ricocheted through my head as the back of my skull hit the ground. The wine bottle thudded against my chest.

Dying's strange when you're aware it's happening. As I stared at the ceiling, willing my fingers to rigour mortis around that bottleneck so it wouldn't slip out of my hand and shatter, I was acutely aware of every part of my life force - blood, breath, future - seeping out of me. Again. In its place I was filled with a sadness and rage that would have condemned me to haunt Jackson, not as a concerned friend but as an irrational spectre of stolen dreams, had the room not collapsed around me before I could commit.

The hallway slipped away, the wall ten feet from me, then a hundred, folding down toward the horizon while every display case and bulletin board faded. Pure white, an infinite and unmoving sea, gradually dimming from grey to black. For an instant I was bodiless, suspended in shadow, and then the lights flickered on.

I was standing behind a podium, facing endless rows of empty benches. I could see the three walls bordering the seating, their grey-blue paint and framed photos of luminaries, their exit signs and bathroom doors, but whenever I tried to count the number of pews, estimate the size of this hall, the floor seemed to extend, new rows popping up. A closed casket was set off to the side, dark and angular, black veneer gleaming like a vintage Cadillac. Bouquets of pink and purple wildflowers surrounded it as if standing guard. Programs on quilted paper were scattered throughout the pews, no mourners present to read them.

My own private funeral. Or was it Adrienne's?

I laughed. Why would this be anyone's but mine? This was my life, after all.

"Last time, I nit-picked all the eulogies," I said into the mic, my voice reverberating across the hall and disappearing, no echo. "But now that I'm up here, and I'm at a loss."

As I spoke, I noticed a single person in one of the pews, five rows down and far to the right. The stranger was thin and unobtrusive, cloaked in black lace. I could detect pallor behind the veil, but its face was hidden from me.

Does Death look like us? I wondered. Or are we escorted off this plane, at the end of it all, by a robed skeleton with empty eyes and a rictus grin? I hoped it was the latter.

In any case, the visitor was in no rush to hook me off the stage and drag me into the afterlife, so I continued.

"I never understood how we expect people to give eulogies, anyway. How is it possible for anyone – let alone a grieving loved one – to summarize a whole person in a few minutes?"

The eyes of the casket photo bored into me. A cap-and-gown yearbook picture, posed and impersonal.

"In any case, my parents weren't bullshitting. I am generous, intelligent, passionate about the people I love. I'm creative, I have an offbeat way of seeing the world, and I can appreciate people with all their quirks and idiosyncrasies. I like to use humour to cheer people up, but the problem with that is not everyone gets my humour."

I paused for the muted funeral giggles, which of course never came.

"I'm very chill, until I'm not. By that I mean, I sometimes tried to be so easy-going that I didn't advocate for myself, until eventually I'd hit a boiling point and blow up over something inconsequential. I also had this tendency to over-apologize even though I wasn't actually trying to take accountability, I was angling to be reassured. In that regard, I cared a lot about what other people thought of me. I think I had it in the back of my head that people would turn on me if I inconvenienced them."

The words spilled out like a waterfall, no one there to stop or console me.

"I was ride-or-die loyal to my friends, but I had a jealous streak. There was no ulterior motive behind that, I just wanted to be everyone's favourite. I wanted think someone saw something special in me."

The draped figure squirmed, as if uncomfortable with my candour.

"I wanted to have this teen movie high school experience, find a group of weirdos just like me that I could fit myself into. I'm not sure I ever accomplished that. Don't get me wrong, I had lots of friends – I was a nice person, I was likeable – but I'm not sure I ever opened myself up to others."

These things used to pain me, but as I said them out loud, all I felt was indifference. Like I'd cut open my heart and dust had coughed out. It wasn't a bad feeling, though. Not apathy, but peace.

"I spent my school years thinking I was waiting for the freedom to be more fully myself. You could say that day never came. But I guess that imperfect, insecure, hot-tempered person was me. Maybe I've been my full self this whole time. And that's fine, because I was also all the nice things my parents and friends said in their eulogies."

Life had been good. Death was good, too. Freed of my worldly constraints, had I done anything differently? I read strange books and listened to loud music and hung out with a small handful of people with whom I'd shared common interests.

Shoulders hitching, the stranger swept its veil aside to wipe away a tear. It was Adrienne, morgue pale, her weeping giving her Alice Cooper eyes. My navel-gazing had resonated with her. We shared a lingering look of understanding which Adrienne seemed to wilt under. Then, she pounced on me.

The room had previously stretched to confound me; now it shrank, delivering Adrienne from a distant pew to the pulpit in a flurry of midnight black fabric. Draping robes became the slashing wings of crows as she knocked me down, kicking my shins and clawing my eyes. Her garments moved of their own volition to envelop me, restraining my arms, tangling around my legs, forcing their way inside my mouth and down my throat. I gagged on the veil, the reflex almost enough to dislodge it. But the veil fought back, delicate lace unravelling and sprouting barbs that latched onto the walls of my airway. Copper flooded my tastebuds when I coughed.

This was the kiss Nyhiloteph had threatened me with, bloody and ruinous. Agony convulsed me. Adrienne, still writhing on top of me, shoved my head down, pushing me deeper beneath her folds even as they continued to burrow into every orifice, plugging my nostrils and blinding my eyes. A tendril tickled my inner ears just before the drums burst. My world was nothing but darkness and cacophony.

The back of my head – Adrienne's head – whoever's head smacked against the wall. Dots like gnats flitted across my line of vision, before being scattered by another a wave of pain. My eyes stared straight ahead, fixed on other people's trophies. The knife in my chest jiggled. I tried to move out of the way (of what?) but couldn't so much as twitch with Adrienne's body. It was useless now, at least for me. The knife fell into my lap. The tear it left in

Adrienne's shirt ripped wider, and the flaps around the wound parted. Someone was fighting for this body.

Adrienne wanted to live. And maybe she would. Perhaps, after everything, she would be a miracle. I would have let go, let her in, if it weren't for the wine bottle in her hands. Maybe she'd seen through Nyhiloteph – when we locked eyes at the psychic funeral, I truly believed we were on the same page. But she was clearly taking some inspiration from him.

No sensation came to me from her hands anymore, so I didn't feel her grip slacken, the vessel rolling out of her palm, until the bottle was floating in front of my face, held up by an invisible hand. Jackson stared at it in wordless horror, like he'd already forgotten the weirder wonders he'd witnessed. My vision was limited by human eyes, so I risked a partial emergence from my shell, peeking out to see Artemis standing between us. Adrienne picked that moment for her big push, just as Artemis reached out and took my hand.

I fought Artemis' grip as the scene hazed over, thinking the hallway was filling with smoke. But the hallway was fine. I was just losing the ability to see it.

A familiar voice cut through my fog. "Holy -"

And then another I recognized: "Oh fuck!"

And lastly, even softer, a girlish, soupy cough.

Abdul was lifting Jackson by the shoulders, spiriting him away from the crime scene, doubling back to retrieve the knife. Brady stayed with Adrienne, pressing down on her wound and murmuring consolations.

Artemis grabbed my chin, turning my head away. "Nothing more you can do here," he said. Something I wished I'd learned a long time ago. I hazarded one final glance to see my friends disappearing into the mist.

Or, I guess that was me disappearing.

Chapter 45

OTTAWA – A high school senior stabbed in the chest during the Tom Thomson 'Grad Oscars' massacre is awake and in stable condition.

A blade barely missed the heart of 18-year-old Adrienne De Keyser after chaos broke out during an awards ceremony at her west end high school. The bizarre incident, which is still under investigation, left 13 students and 3 faculty members dead.

A family spokesperson says De Keyser has no memory of the event and was unable to identify her attacker. She's currently "focusing on healing mentally and physically" and has been enjoying visits with her boyfriend and other survivors.

"Adrienne has weathered more tragedy than most in the last few months, which is saying something in this community."

The honour roll student is the daughter of two well-known philanthropists who were reported missing in an unrelated case...

Epilogue: Nocturnal Pleasure

There is a house, on the last street before the neighbourhood breaks into woods, where a skeleton sits on the roof. The skeleton is plastic, dressed up in seasonal garb; the building is a chiropractor's clinic.

The house next to it is haunted.

Bad things have happened in this neighbourhood, closer to home, but those were Tragedies. At school, the faces of the dead stare down at you from the walls, looking too human, too much like you do, now. The same faces once laid out alongside inky headlines: *No Charges Laid in "Mass Hysteria" Murders. Decades later, still no justice for survivors.* Even if you aren't moved by the sight of them, you can't joke about their fates; not if you don't want your mom to start crying, or a teacher who lived through it to upbraid you. These dead, even twenty years on, must be respected.

What happened in this house was different. No one mourned the man who died here. Maybe that's why he clings to the place so tightly.

They say police who investigated the bizarre slaying didn't like to set foot in the building, even long after the body had been carted away. When the old store was finally sold, the new owner was conked with a falling beam the moment he entered. The building was sold again. Same deal. When a developer tried to demolish it, there were accidents on the construction site, equipment tampered with, operators who swore they'd seen a bloodied man who stared at them, then vanished. Eventually the union refused to send workers.

And so, the house stands empty. A campfire myth, a dare.

Under the failing light of the waning moon, a pair of boys wrench open the rotting door with a borrowed crowbar.

"Is that where they bashed his head in?"

"Right there. They say you can still see the blood stains on the floorboards."

The adventurers get what they came for - books decaying on shelves, cobwebs stuck to ceilings, a general aura of neglect - and something they didn't. On one of the high shelves sits a wine bottle, glowing faintly even though no light shines upon it.

Standing on tiptoes, the bolder boy reaches to grab it, and feels a cold hand grasp his wrist. In his ear, a voice like rustling spiders hisses, Don't touch. The boy staggers backwards, looking around.

"What happened?" his friend asks.

"I don't know. I felt someth..."

He doesn't finish the sentence. The atmosphere in the room changes, crackling with a strange energy. Lights no longer hooked to electricity flicker on, sagging books stand upright, grotesque masks watch them from walls. Above their heads, an owl hoots.

And in the air, not in one place but everywhere, two distinct voices, laughing at them.

The boys leave without a souvenir. Behind them, the store falls dark.

Inside, a record starts spinning of its own accord: David Bowie crooning "Drive-In Saturday." If the raiders had looked over their shoulders at any point in their mad dash to the car, they would have seen unnatural colours appear between the boards that block the bay window.

The Grimoire lit up like a juke box.

The End

Acknowledgements:

It's been amazing to work with Little Ghosts Books, who have contributed so much to the indie horror scene in Canada and beyond. I can't overstate how much better this book became after Chris got his hands on it. He identified the beating heart of the story and encouraged me to dig deeper into the characters, translating teen angst into a compelling emotional arc.

My Ottawa writing friends Chris Campeau, Steve Smith, and Ben Cirne gave great advice and feedback (as they always do) as I was shaping the story. (Apologies to the restaurant patrons who were seated next to our group while we dissected some of the more gruesome sequences.)

Thank you to Monica Singh, Kirsten Aucoin and Krista Marie, who not only agreed to beta-read 40,000 words for a stranger but gave incredibly helpful comments.

Ever grateful to Kristian McKesey, for being a voice of reason and for years of aimless drives.

Much love to my brother Alexander and my parents, Colin and Erin, who fostered my lifelong love of reading and writing and also indulged my youthful macabre streak. (They were also the ones who got me into Meat Loaf, so really, this book is their fault).

Cheers to the horror scene, especially the indie, experimental, and bizarro writers and publishers who continue to hop the fences, enter new worlds, and bring back shadowy, hungry, fanged things. Thanks also to everyone involved in the production of The Evil Dead, Dazed and Confused, Ichi the Killer, Adventureland, the Chucky franchise, Mean Girls, and the unGoogleable horror comedy Porno, which were all huge influences. And to the late, great Anne Rice, from whom I stole the "telepathic, semi-omniscient first person narrator" trick.

Rest in peace Jim Steinman and Meat Loaf, who gave this melancholy, melodramatic book an epic soundtrack.

Author

Madison McSweeney writes occult horror and bizarro.

She's the author of The Doom That Came to Mellonville, the novelettes Beach Vibes and The Forest Dreams With Teeth, and the gothic poetry collection Fringewood. She blogs about horror for Divination Hollow Reviews and occasionally draws things.

In her spare time, she's probably binging cult films or walking aimlessly through Ottawa, daydreaming to heavy metal.

Find her at www.madisonmcsweeney.com and Twitter/X @MMcSw13.